U0043174

讀李家同學英文 1

李家同◎著

Nick Hawkins（郝凱揚）◎翻譯　　周正一◎解析

My
Blind Mentor
我的盲人恩師

序

　　我真該謝謝郝凱揚先生將我的文章譯成了英文。這當然不是一件簡單的事情，但是我看了他的翻譯，我發現他的翻譯是絕對正確的，而且非常優美。郝先生是美國人，能做這件事情，充分展現他的中文造詣很高，他一定是一位非常聰明的人。

　　這一本書最大的好處是有對英文的註解、也有練習，想學英文的年輕人可以從註解中學到很多英文的基本學問。我在此給讀者一個建議：你不妨先看看中文文章，先不看英文的翻譯，然後試著將中文翻成英文，我相信你一定會覺得中翻英好困難。翻完以後，再去看郝先生的翻譯，相信你可以學到不少。

　　我尤其希望讀者注意標點符號的用法。英文的標點符號是非常重要的，中文句子對標點符號的標準比較寬鬆，但英文絕對不行，一個標點符號用錯了，全句的結構就是錯了。讀者可以利用這個機會好好地學會如何正確地下英文的標點符號。

　　另外，正如郝先生所建議的，千萬要注意動詞的用法，如果你英文動詞沒有錯，你的英文就很厲害了。信不信由你，英文不好的人常常不會用現在完成式，可是這本書裡用了很多的現在完成式，你不妨仔細研究為什麼要用這種我們中國人所不熟悉的時態。

　　在英文句子裡，一定要有一個主詞和一個動詞，讀者不妨在每一

個句子裡去找一下，主詞和動詞一定會存在。我們中國人有時會寫一個英文句子，但是句子中，主詞和動詞弄不清楚，以至於有的動詞沒有主詞。也就因為如此，凡是這種主詞和動詞關係不清楚的句子，意思也會弄不清楚。讀者如果覺得這些文章很容易懂，其實完全是因為每一個句子的主詞和動詞都很清楚的原因。

　　最後我謝謝周先生，他的註解使這本書生色不少。當然我也該謝謝聯經出版公司，我相信這本書的出版會有助於很多想學好英文的年輕人，這本書能夠順利出現，林載爵先生和何采嬪女士有很大的功勞，我在此謝謝他們。

李家同

閱讀本書的理想方式

有機會翻譯李家同的作品實在是我的榮幸！他不僅是個好作家，更是一個好人，所以他的故事有一種真誠、由衷的感覺。他儉樸的文風毫無炫耀的味道，正好凸顯出內容的精采和寓意的美妙。這種故事就是好看，讀起來又有趣味又有意義——無論是讀英文還是中文的。

「關懷」兩個字是李家同作品最明顯的特色。他有一顆「不忍人之心」：對世上不幸的人充滿了愛與同情。他的博愛精神顯然源自於他的宗教信仰，但他的人道主義是每位讀者都能欣賞的，不管自己信不信教。（我信的教和他不一樣，不過我還是很認同他的思想。）尤其值得我們學習的是，他胸懷世界：他的關切沒有國界——光是這幾篇文章就提到英國人、日本人、台灣人、非洲人、美國人、歐洲人、印度人和巴西人。如果我們像李家同所鼓勵我們的那樣，夷平我們心中的高牆，我相信我們的愛也會跨越文化間的隔閡和種族間的摩擦。

我很感謝李家同寫這些故事。我從中得到了極大的收穫。

我的翻譯原則

在翻譯的過程當中，我最重視的是保持每篇故事原有的風格，所以我並沒有一個字一個字的翻譯。有些中文的說法，尤其是俚語和成語，是沒有英文翻譯的；這類情況時，我常常得調整句子的結構。比

方說，英文對於文法和標點符號的要求比中文要來得嚴。李家同喜歡寫比較長的句子，但這種習慣不符合英文的文法，所以我縮短了很多句子，同時也加進了一些標點符號。要記得，英文跟中文表達的方法本來就大不相同，所以太直接地翻譯往往不會有很好的結果。

閱讀本書的理想方式

許多台灣人學英文，用的方法是死記硬背，今天背文法、明天背單字。我並不否認背是很重要的技巧，可是那絕不是閱讀這本書的理想方式。為什麼呢？因為這不是英文課本，乃是文學，而文學是要享受的，不是要死背的。當你認真閱讀的時候，你自然而然地會吸收有用的生詞。**你並不需要看得懂每個字或徹底了解每個句子的文法。**有些詞是很少用的，所以你不必全背。可是，假如你一再看到某一個詞或句型，你自然而然會記住。真的想好好從中學習的話，我建議，當你有機會的時候，試著用你學到的生詞與句型來造句，或用在你日常生活的英文對話中。語言是要用的，不然很容易忘記。

當你閱讀時，我建議你注意以下幾個重點：

- **動詞的時態。**不同時態之間的差別有時候很明顯，有時候很細微，但是都很重要。舉例來說，從「我的媽媽來看我」這個標題你看不出時態來。請問，應該用過去式把它譯為 My mom came to see me，還是用現在式寫 My mom comes to see me？這就要看內容。如果故事寫的是敘述者本身的媽媽來看他，就應該用現在式。但由於標題指的媽媽其實是另一個人物的媽媽，標題等於是那個人說的話，而在他說這話的時候，他媽媽已經來過了，所以要用過去式。

- **冠詞**。基本上，用 the 表示你是特別指某一個東西，如 the bottle is on the table，或是說這個東西只有一個，如 the earth is round。世界上的瓶子很多，可是你指的這個瓶子因為某某原因而跟別的瓶子不一樣——可能是你給媽媽買的或是你要請人家喝的。相對的，如果你說 a bottle is on the table，那就表示桌子上的是個普普通通的瓶子。但不管怎樣，你總不能說 bottle is on the table，因為 bottle 前面一定要有冠詞才可以用在句子裡。在標題裡面，冠詞尤其重要：比方說，The perfect day 表示這十全十美的一天只有一個，或是它有某某特色。假如那個標題改譯為A perfect day，意思就不符合故事的內容。

- **中文的慣用說法英文怎麼說**。英文沒有「爽」這個字，所以「我感到特別的爽」這句要怎麼翻譯呢？我發揮了一點創意，把它翻成了 I felt like a million dollars，因為這句道地的英文剛好表達相同的意思。另外，李家同的人物常說「老王」、「小李」之類的小名來稱呼熟人，可是美國人沒有這樣的習慣。怎麼辦呢？很簡單，就直接翻譯：Old Wang, Little Lee等等。這樣讀者就知道這是中國人的習慣，而故事加上了一個中國文化的味道。

- **如何用文法和標點符號來創造戲劇效果**。我在上面說過，英文對文法及標點符號的要求比中文要來得嚴。對我來講，這其實是好事，因為文法跟標點符號是極好的表達工具。例如，「我的盲人恩師」的第一段中文都是一個句子，其後半為「他是一個完完全全的盲人，對外界任何的亮光，都已沒有反應，經年生活在黑暗中」。看看英文的標點符號如何給這個句子添上一些色彩：He is totally blind— no form of external light produces any reaction in him. He has lived in darkness for years. 在本書裡，這樣的例子多得不得了，所以要注意。

學會感受到一個外語的節奏，尤其是一個跟自己的母語大相逕庭的外語，絕非一夕之功。你要多聽、多看、多想，才會有感覺。假如你看了一次之後還是不太懂，千萬不要氣餒！繼續努力。雖然你也許會覺得自己的英文不夠好，我還是建議你不要太依賴中文。當然，你可以先瀏覽中文的故事，再來讀英文的翻譯，如此你就比較容易推測你不懂的地方在寫什麼。但更好的方法是，先整個讀英文，再以中文確認你的理解是否正確。

如果你的聽力很強，你可以試著先聽錄音，再看故事；要不然可以等到看了以後再聽。但無論如何一定要聽，因為唯有仔細聽，才能抓住語感。而且誰都知道，學一種語言要模仿那些講得比你流利的人；多聽標準的英文會幫助你說更標準的英文。

總之，請好好享受吧！不管是中文英文，他們都是很棒的故事！

郝凱揚

選列單字的原則

常用而又重要的單字

我們主張學習英文應該善用工具書——如字典和文法書。學生應該有動手勤查字典的習慣，在這方面，一本內容豐富、解說詳盡的英英或英漢字典比電子字典更好。從查字典的過程中體會字義和用法，是讓英文進步的不二法門。所以在編寫每一章的字彙時，我們不師法字典，將所有的單字全部臚列；反之，我們以過來人的經驗，從譯文裡挑選出重要實用而且是學習者在使用字典時仍會困惑或感到困難的字。因此挑選單字時，常用和重要就是我們依據的兩大準則。

一字多義，以原著和譯文為主

一個單字經常有多種含意，如何抉擇取捨常是學習者、尤其是初學者苦惱的事。在這方面我們的編寫原則是：以原著和譯文為依憑。

除了一字多義，另外還有一字多性(詞性)的問題。以〈荒原之旅〉第四段最後一句 "...the British moorland still holds a very powerful allure... 為例，其中的 allure 一字常常作動詞使用，但在英譯裡顯然是作名詞用，在編寫上我們就把它標示為名詞。

還有些字，特別是過去分詞如：restrained, afflicted等，用法已經

相當接近形容詞，我們就把它當成形容詞(adj.)註解。

為了區分副詞(adv.)和形容詞(adj.)，副詞的中譯採用「……地」，例如 sparsely(稀疏地)。而形容詞的中譯則採用「……的」，例如 desolate(冷清的；荒涼的)。

從中等程度學生的角度出發

學習英文當然單字記得愈多愈好(The more, the better.)但是依讀者本身程度，選擇適合自己學習能力範圍內、並適合自己需求的單字來記，才能事半功倍。硬要初學者去記像「百科全書」(encyclopedia)、「心理學」(psychology)、「二氧化碳」(carbon dioxide)、「盲腸」(appendix)等較為艱澀的字，實在是毫無意義可言。在這方面，我們還是根據經驗法則，把一位中等程度的高中生或社會人士所應該要具備的單字整理出來，做詞性分析和最基本的意義解說。雖然我們一直期望讀者能親自動手翻查字典來學習英文，但是為了讓您閱讀得更順暢，我們仍然隨頁提供了字彙表，希望能給學習者更好的學習效果。

周正一

目次
CONTENTS

iii 　序／李家同

v 　閱讀本書的理想方式／郝凱揚

ix 　選列單字的原則／周正一

1 　My Blind Mentor
　　我的盲人恩師

37 　"My Mom Came to See Me"—a true story
　　「我的媽媽來看我」——一個真實的故事

67 　Journey to the Moorland
　　荒原之旅

105 　Chef Wu's Feast
　　吳師傅的盛宴

117　The Perfect Day
　　　十全十美的一天

133　Let the Wall Fall:
　　　－Reflections on meeting Mother Teresa
　　　讓高牆倒下吧——訪問德蕾莎修女的感想

My Blind Mentor

我的盲人恩師

1-5　　　我的博士論文指導教授師雷格教授是麻省理工學院的數學博士，現在是明尼蘇達大學的計算機科學講座教授，他是一個完完全全的盲人，對外界任何的亮光，都已沒有反應，經年生活在黑暗之中。

　　可是我的老闆（我們念博士學位時，都將指導教授稱之為老闆），卻又是一位非常溫和，而且性情平和的人，見過他的人，都會發現他從未對他的失明有任何自怨自艾，更沒有因此而脾氣不好。

　　其實做一個盲人，不是一件容易的事，兩年以前我的老闆來清華，住進我們的招待所，我必須牽著他到處摸索，使他知道馬桶在哪裡，洗臉盆在哪裡，肥皂在哪裡，冷氣機如何開關，早上吃飯的地方如何走等等。我後來問他，如果他住進一家旅舍沒有人指點他，他如何知道這些？他說通常人家看到他是瞎子，都會設法帶他摸一遍，如果無人帶領，他差不多要花上一個小時才能搞清楚東南西北。

　　大家一定好奇，我的老闆是怎樣念書的？在上課的時候，他和同學一樣坐在下面，老師知道他是瞎子，因此在黑板上寫的時候，一概特

CD1-4　◇ thesis adviser 論文指導老師　　　　◇ external（adj.）外部的；外在的

My former Ph.D. thesis adviser, Professor Slagle, has a doctorate degree in mathematics from MIT and is currently a chair professor of computer science at the University of Minnesota. He is totally blind— no form of external light produces any reaction in him. He has lived in darkness for years.

But my boss (we all called our advisers bosses while studying for our Ph.D.s) is a very gentle, contented man by nature. Anyone who meets him will discover he has never been bitter about his lack of sight, nor has he ever let it make him ill-tempered.

In all honesty, though, being a blind man is no easy thing. Two years ago my boss came to Tsing Hua University, where he stayed in the guest reception building. I had to lead him around by the hand so he could feel where the toilet was, where the face-washing basin was, where the soap was, how to turn the air conditioner on and off, where to go for breakfast in the morning, and so on. Afterward I asked him, if he stayed in a motel where no one showed him around, how did he learn all this? He said that usually people would see he was blind and make an effort to lead him around to get a feel for the place. If no one guided him, it would take him about an hour to figure out where everything was.

All of you are probably wondering, how did my boss get through school? During class, he would sit down with the other students. The teacher knew my boss was blind, so when writing on the blackboard

◇ nature (n.) 本性；天性
◇ bitter (adj.) 忿懣不滿的；內心怨艾的

◇ air conditioner 冷暖氣機

別為他講得比較清楚一點，如果在黑板上劃了圖，更加要特別描述一番。如果他當時不懂，據他說只要下課以後同學們一定都樂於幫忙。

考試只好用口試，他說每位老師都為他而舉行個別的口試，因為他念的是數學，人家一下子就知道他的思路是否合乎邏輯，口試並非難事。

6-10　如何看書呢？我的老闆完全靠聽錄音帶，美國有一個盲人錄音服務社的非營利性組織，任何盲人要念哪一本書，這個組織就找人替他念，義工奇多無比，大多數義工要等很久才輪到他念一本書。可是內行人都知道，現在做研究，最重要的還是要看論文，我老闆在麻省理工學院念博士的時候，就常常貼出佈告，說他要看哪一篇論文，希望有人替他念，當時麻省理工學院的計算機研究生，幾乎都替他念過，現在在伊利諾州立大學教書的劉炯朗教授，就替他念過。研究生念論文，除了出於愛心以外，還有一個原因。等於自己也念了一篇論文。

◇ detailed（adj.）詳盡的；仔細的　　　　◇ sound（adj.）完整的；健全的
◇ audiotape（n.）錄音帶（註：錄影帶為 videotape，在科技精進，高科技產品推陳出新的時代，這兩樣東西都已經快從生活中絕跡。）

he would always explain a bit more clearly for his benefit. If the teacher drew a diagram on the board, he would have to give a particularly detailed description. If my boss didn't understand right away, his classmates, he said, would be glad to help him once class was over.

When he took tests, he had to take them orally. He said every teacher would give him an individualized oral test. Because he studied math, they would immediately know whether or not his line of reasoning was logically sound, so the tests weren't too difficult.

How did he read books? My boss relied completely on audiotapes. 6-10 In the US there's a nonprofit organization that provides recording services for the blind. When any blind person wants to read a book, this organization will find someone to read it for him. There are incredibly many volunteers there, so many that most of them have to wait a long time before it's their turn to read a book. Any insider knows, though, that the key to modern research is reading papers. While my boss was a Ph.D. student at MIT, he would often post a notice saying he needed to read a certain article and hoped that someone would read it for him. Nearly all the computer science students who were then at MIT read at least one paper for him, including Professor C. L. Liu, who currently teaches at Illinois State. In addition to doing it out of love, the students had another reason to read: it meant they would get to read an article for themselves as well.

◇ volunteer(n.)義工　　　　　◇ post(v.)張貼

美國曾經通過一個聯邦法案，規定這一類錄音帶和書的郵寄，一概免貼郵票，否則我想他不可能念到這麼多的書。

懂得計算機科學的人，一定更會好奇地想知道盲人如何寫計算機程式？如何從程式中尋找錯誤？

我老闆念書是三十年前的事，當時計算機沒有任何一樣替盲人著想的設備，因此他寫好了程式(用點字機寫)，就念給一位同學聽，總有人肯替他打成卡片，然後替他送給計算機中心。

他拿到計算機印出來的結果，又要找一位同學念給他聽，他只好根據聽到的結果，決定要如何改，也總有同學肯接受他的卡片，而替他改幾張卡片。

最近美國已有不少替盲人設計的終端機，盲人要修改程式，據說一點問題也沒有，我的老闆說明尼蘇達大學有很多位盲人學生，其中不少都是學理工的，全部都要用計算機的終端機。

11-15　我老闆一直認為盲人應該和平常人一樣地生活，社會不該歧視盲人，可是也不該對盲人過分地大驚小怪。兩年以前，我陪我老闆到桃

◇ stipulate(v.)(法律)明文規定　　　　◇ revise(v.)修訂；修正
◇ program(n.)(電腦)程式　　　　　　◇ computer terminal 電腦終端機

An American federal law stipulates that books and tapes for this purpose can be mailed without stamps. Otherwise, I don't think he could possibly have read so many books.

Those who understand computer science will be more curious to know how a blind man could write computer programs. How could he find the bugs in his code?

My boss studied thirty years ago, back when there was no computer equipment designed for the blind. Hence, after he wrote a program (using a Braille typewriter), he would read it to a classmate. There would always be someone willing to put it onto a card for him and take it to the computer center. After the computer printed out the program results, he would have to find another classmate to read them to him, whereupon he would have to decide how to revise the code based on what he had heard. Once again, there would always be a student willing to pick up or change his cards for him.

CD1-2

Recently America has developed quite a few computer terminals designed for the blind. I've heard that editing programs is now no problem at all for them. My boss says there are a lot of blind students at Minnesota, many of whom study science and engineering. All of them use these terminals for computing.

My boss has always thought that the blind should live like ordinary people. Society shouldn't discriminate against them, but it shouldn't

11-15

◇ ordinary (adj.) 一般的；平常的　　◇ discriminate (against) (v.) 歧視

園機場搭機回美國，機場的某航空公司辦事員發現他是盲人，大為緊張，問他在洛杉磯有沒有人接，因為他在洛杉磯機場要轉飛機，我老闆說沒有人接，某航空公司因此堅持不肯讓他上機，他們說他們不敢負這個責任，最後還是由我出面，由老闆簽了一份文件，保證不會告某航空公司，某航空公司才肯讓他上機。

事後我老闆告訴我，他常搭乘飛機去旅行，從來沒有碰到這種事，他說英國機場對盲人招待最好，他們一看到有盲人，會立刻請他到貴賓室去，而且會有人帶他去登機，某航空公司雖然關心他的安全，都沒有派人帶路，大概他們知道自己不會被告，也就不管這位盲人的安全了。

我老闆說他什麼交通工具都用過，從來沒有人接，火車、地下鐵等等他都一個人坐，從來沒有人拒絕他上去，在他看來，這種所謂的關懷，其實根本是歧視。

◇ accompany (v.) 陪同；伴隨　　　◇ intercede (v.) 從中說情；居間疏通
◇ grounds (n.) 理由；根據　　　　◇ sue (v.) 控告；對 (某人) 提出告訴

make too big a fuss over them either. Two years ago, I accompanied my boss to the Taoyuan airport for his flight back to America. An employee of a certain airline there got very nervous after discovering he was blind and asked him if anyone would meet him in Los Angeles, where he had to change planes. My boss said no one would. As a result, the airline utterly refused to let him on the airplane on the grounds that they were unwilling to accept responsibility if anything were to happen to him. Only after I interceded and my boss signed a document promising not to sue the airline would they finally let him on his flight.

Afterward, my boss told me that he regularly travels by air, but that sort of thing had never happened to him before. He said airports in England treat blind people the best. The moment they see anyone who's blind, they'll invite him to the VIP lounge, and when it's time to board, they'll have someone escort him onto the plane. Although the airline in Taoyuan cared about his safety, they didn't send anyone to escort him. They probably stopped caring about his safety once they knew they wouldn't get sued.

My boss says he's used about every means of transportation there is without ever asking anyone to pick him up. He's ridden trains, subways, etc. on his own without anyone ever refusing to let him on. In his opinion, this so-called consideration is really nothing more than discrimination.

◇ VIP lounge 貴賓室

◇ escort (v.) 護衛；護送

◇ discrimination (n.) 歧視

我們中國人喜將盲人講得可憐兮兮的，我曾在台灣聽過一個來自香港的盲人青年合唱團演唱，演唱中一再強調他們都是中國內亂的犧牲品，所唱的歌也都是天倫淚之類的歌，真是賺人熱淚。

可是我去了美國，碰到了我的老闆，以後又碰到了若干盲人學者，才發現盲洋人從不爭取同情，他們努力地和我們這些人一齊生活，非不得已絕不讓人感到他們是盲人，也無怪乎盲洋人在學術上有傑出表現者多矣。

16-20　　像蘇聯的龐屈耳根博士，就是一個例子，這位蘇聯的數學家，在控制理論上的貢獻，可以說是到了永垂不朽的地步，他從小就瞎了，上課時帶了媽媽去，就靠他媽媽將黑板上的符號、圖等等解釋給他聽，其實他媽媽根本不懂數學，有時候大概都講錯了。我在美國念書的時候，曾見到這位大師演講，他大概是用俄文演講，替他翻譯的是一位波蘭的教授，此公奇壞無比，平時對我們同學甚為嚴格，是一位不受同學歡迎的教授，那天他大概翻譯得不太對，被那位大師用英文臭罵，我到現在還清楚記得那位盲人大師的威風。

◇ abject(adj.)可憐的；悲慘的
◇ sort(n.)(某一類型的)人(註：亦可使用type)
◇ manufacture(v.)生產；製造
◇ strive(v.)努力；積極想要……
◇ achieve(v.)獲致；達成

We Chinese like to think of the blind as abject and pitiful. I once heard a blind youth choir from Hong Kong perform in Taiwan. As they sang, they repeatedly emphasized that they were victims of China's internal strife, and their songs were all of a sentimental, teary-eyed sort. What a way to manufacture sympathy!

But after I went to America, met my boss, and later met a number of blind scholars, I discovered that blind Westerners never seek for sympathy. They strive to live alongside us, refusing to let other people be conscious of their blindness unless it's absolutely necessary. No wonder there are many blind foreigners who achieve outstanding academic success.

Take Dr. Poutriagon of the USSR, for example. This Soviet 　16-20
mathematician's contributions to control theory will be remembered forever, yet he has been blind since childhood. He used to take his mother to class and rely on her to explain the symbols, figures and so forth on the chalkboard. Actually, his mother didn't know much about math, so she probably got things mixed up a lot of the time. While I was a student in America, I once heard this great scholar lecture, presumably in Russian. The translator was a Polish professor, an exceptionally surly fellow, very strict with us students, whom we heartily detested. That day he was soundly rebuked in English by Poutriagon, probably because his translation was shoddy. Even now I still distinctly remember the commanding presence of that blind scholar.

◇ figure (n.) 圖形　　　　　　　◇ distinctly (adv.) 清楚地；分明地
◇ detest (v.) 厭惡；痛恨

　　我還認識一位盲人，此人生下來就是瞎子，後來成了數學博士，和我是同行，有一次我們同行開會，他應邀在晚間的宴會上致詞，大家以為他會談些學問，不料他大談和芝加哥黑道賭撲克的經驗，試想和黑道賭錢已是有趣的事，而他又是瞎子，所有亮出來的牌全靠人家告訴他，他自己暗的牌是什麼，也靠黑道上的人告訴他，他一口咬定黑道賭博其實並沒有騙局，其理由是他同時和誠實的朋友賭，發現兩者平均輸贏一樣，因此他和芝加哥那批黑道上的人賭了好幾年。

　　為什麼他後來洗手不幹呢？說來有趣，他有一次輕鬆地埋怨一句，說他有一位賭友不夠意思，賭輸了卻遲遲不還他錢，和他賭錢的道上人物立刻拍胸膛，保證替他將錢要回來，我的盲人朋友聽了以後，再也不敢和這些太講義氣的傢伙來往了。

　　現在看看我們國家是怎麼回事？我發現我們整個社會都低估了殘障者的能力，因此如果孩子是個盲人，父母認為他學到了一種謀生的技藝，已經是謝天謝地，我們負責這方面教育的啟聰啟明學校，也作如

◇ conference (n.) 會議
◇ evening banquet 晚宴
◇ gangster (n.) 幫派分子

◇ adamant ['ædəmənt] (adj.) 堅定的；不為所動的
◇ gambling buddies 賭友

I know another blind man who was sightless from the day he was born. He earned a Ph.D. in math and went into the same field as me. Once we went to a conference together and he was invited to speak at the evening banquet. Everyone thought he would talk about something academic, but instead, much to their surprise, he told all about his experiences playing poker with Chicago gangsters. Now, gambling with gangsters is interesting enough in itself, but since he was blind, not only did he depend on the others to tell him what cards were showing, but he had to rely on another gangster to find out what his own hidden cards were as well. He was adamant that the gangsters didn't cheat, for at that time he also gambled with honest friends, and his average winnings and losses were the same with both groups. Thus, he gambled with those gangsters for quite a few years.

Why did he eventually quit? It's actually a funny story: one time he casually complained that one of his gambling buddies was delinquent— he had owed him money for a long time but never paid up. One of the gangsters he was playing with immediately slapped himself on the chest and promised to get the money back for him. After my blind friend heard this, he no longer dared to associate with these guys who were so fiercely loyal to each other.

Now look at the way things are in our country. I've come to realize `CD2-3` that our entire society underestimates the ability of the handicapped. Hence, if a child is blind, his parents are infinitely grateful if he just learns some skill good enough to make a living. Those in charge

◇ delinquent(adj.)為非作歹的；犯罪的
◇ loyal(adj.)忠心耿耿的
◇ underestimate(v.)低估
◇ handicapped(adj.)殘障的

此想，所以念了啟明啟聰學校的盲人學生，是不可能以後念台大電機系或是台大資訊系的。

如果我們要改革，要從觀念改起，我們一定要使失明的年輕人能進入建中，或是一女中，和一般同學一齊生活，學一樣的課程，將來一樣地進入大學，和我們一樣地拿到學位。可惜我們社會上有一批人真死腦筋，只要一點點小小的身體上的缺陷，常常就不能進入某種職業，比方說有一些師範學院拒收有色盲的人，理由是小學老師要帶小孩子過馬路，如果色盲，如何辨認紅綠燈？這種想法，使我國的殘障同胞吃了大虧。

21-25　我希望以後整個社會知道，事實證明盲人可以和我們一樣地念大學，先進國家大學裡盲人比比皆是，也可以拿到博士學位，更可以在事業上做得很成功，我們不該設了很多障礙，使他們根本就進不了中學，更何況大學了，可是一方面我們要掃除這些障礙，一方面卻又對

◇ impaired (adj.) 受損的
◇ reform (v.) 改革；革新
◇ close-minded (adj.) 思想封閉的；頑固

不通的
◇ trivial (adj.) 瑣碎的；不足為道的
◇ reject (v.) 拒絕

of the schools for the visually and hearing impaired that educate these children think the same way, so a blind student who graduates from one of these schools is certainly not going to go on to study electronics or information technology at National Taiwan University.

If we want to reform, we should start by changing our way of thinking. We must enable blind students to get into Chien Kuo High School or Taipei First Girls' High School, live alongside their classmates, take the same classes, get into college the same way and earn the same degrees as we do. Unfortunately, there are a lot of close-minded people in our society. As long as you have some trivial physical deficiency, you can't pursue a certain line of work. For instance, some teachers' colleges reject the color-blind because elementary school teachers have to lead kids across the street, but if the teacher is color-blind, how can he tell if the traffic light is red or green? This sort of thinking is a huge hindrance for our disabled compatriots.

I hope our future society will know, experience has proven that blind people can go to college just like we can. At universities in advanced countries, the blind are ubiquitous. They can earn doctorate degrees and be very successful in their careers. We ought not to set up all sorts of obstacles for them so that they can't even get into high school, let alone college. But even as we want to eliminate these

21-25

◇ hindrance (n.) 阻礙；障礙
◇ disabled (adj.) 殘障的；失能的
◇ advanced country 先進國家
◇ ubiquitous [juˋbɪkwətəs] (adj.) 隨處可見的；到處都有的
◇ obstacle (n.) 阻礙；障礙
◇ eliminate (v.) 取消；淘汰

殘障同胞太過於同情，因為太過於同情，事實上就等於歧視，我們應該盡量鼓勵他們自行解決他們的問題，也只有這樣做，才是真正地幫助了殘障同學。

我過去在美國工作的地方，有一個替我們畫圖的部門，有一次我發現這個部門似乎比以前安靜許多，所有的工作人員都不開口講話，而用手語交談，一問之下，才知道他們來了一位聾子的畫圖員，大家就決定學習手語，久而久之養成了習慣，大家都用手語交談了，這是一個典型的例子，充分表示一個團體應該如何接納一位殘障同胞。

有一次我在紐西蘭街上看到一位盲人，我好意問他，要不要我幫忙他過馬路，他笑笑說不必，然後他說聽你的口音，你是外鄉人，如果要找路，可以問他，我當時在找某一路公車，就趁機問他到哪裡去找，在他的指點之下，順利地找到了。

我希望我們的小學、國中、高中以至於大學能夠毫無保留地接受盲人學生，使他們能像普通同學們一樣地接受教育，我也希望，我國的政府機關，不僅不要對殘障同胞的求職設限，而且要定下榜樣，主

◇ sign language 手語　　　　　　　　◇ classic(adj.)經典的；絕好的

obstacles, we give our handicapped comrades too much sympathy, and too much sympathy is really just discrimination. We should encourage them to resolve their problems on their own, for only by so doing can we really help them.

At the place where I used to work in America there was an art department. One time I discovered that the department seemed much quieter than before— none of the employees opened their mouths to speak but communicated in sign language instead. When I asked why, I found out that a deaf artist had come to work with them, so everybody had decided to learn sign language. After a while it became a habit: everyone used sign language to communicate. This is a classic example that vividly illustrates how an organization should accept a disabled colleague.

One time I saw a blind man on the street in New Zealand. Out of kindness, I asked him if he wanted me to help him across the road. He smiled and said there was no need, and then he said that he could tell by my accent I wasn't from around here, so if I needed directions to anywhere I could ask him. I happened to be looking for a certain bus just then, so I took him up on his offer and asked where to find it. With his guidance, I found it without a hitch.

I hope that our elementary schools, middle schools, high schools and colleges will embrace blind students and allow them to receive the same education as their regular classmates. I also hope that our

---

◇ colleague (n.) 同事　　　◇ accent (n.) 口音　　　◇ hitch (n.) 阻撓；不順

動地僱用殘障同胞。至於盲胞在工作以及學習環境中所可能遭遇的問題，政府不必擔心，因為我們應該有信心，那個環境中自然會有善心的人幫助他們解決問題，過度的關心其實也是一種歧視。

◇ government institution(s) 政府機關　　◇ study environment 學習環境

country's government institutions will not only not set limits on what jobs the disabled can hold, but also set an example by actively hiring them. As for the problems our blind compatriots may encounter in their work and study environments, the government need not worry— we ought to have faith that there will be good-hearted people there to help them solve problems. Excessive concern is really just another form of discrimination.

◇ faith (n.) 信心　　　　　◇ excessive (adj.) 過度的

（1）Anyone who... 凡是……的人（2段）

Anyone who meets him will discover he has never been bitter about his lack of sight, nor has he ever let it make him ill-tempered.

見過他的人，都會發現他從未對他的失明有任何自怨自艾，更沒有因此而脾氣不好。

解析

Anyone who... 很趨近中文「凡是……的人」。「凡是愛上帝的人」英文表達成 Anyone who loves God...。所以，以下你會怎麼説呢？

小試身手

1. 凡和他作對的都受到嚴厲的處罰。

　_____

此外原譯文裡有一個很不錯的片語 to be bitter about...，提供大家學習。bitter 在這裡的原義為「怨懟的；心懷怨憎的」，所以整個片語的意思並不難掌握。請做以下練習：

小試身手

2. 他對於所受的冷淡對待心懷怨懟。

　_____

（2）lead... by the hand 拉著（某人）的手引導他（3段）

I had to lead him around by the hand so he could feel where the toilet was, where the face-washing basin was, where the soap was, how to turn the air conditioner on and off, where to go for breakfast in the morning, and so on.

我必須牽著他到處摸索，使他知道馬桶在哪裡，洗臉盆在哪裡，肥皂在哪裡，冷氣機如何開關，早上吃飯的地方如何走等等。

解析

「拉著某人的手引導某人」英文的表達方式為：lead... by the hand。你注意到中文（拉著）這個動作的後面直接就接上（某人的手）。可是英文的習慣不是這樣子的。英文這麼說：「拉著 + 某人 + by the hand」。你得注意介詞 (by) 和定冠詞 (the)。這個句型很重要，提供兩個練習機會給你：

小試身手

3.　他一把抓住我的臂膀。（提示：grab... by the arm）

_____

4.　我一拳打在他肚子上。（註：套用武俠小說的寫法：我朝他肚子就是一拳；提示：punch... stomach）。

_____

國中生學過 turn on（打開）和 turn off（關掉）這兩個片語。其實介詞 on 本身就有「開」的意思，而 off 則為「關」的意思。挑戰以下：

小試身手

5.　他們的愛情時斷時續了六年。

_____

（3）figure out 瞭解；弄清楚（3段）

If no one guided him, it would take him about an hour to figure out where everything was.

如果無人帶領，他差不多要花上一個小時才能搞清楚東西南北。

解析

figure out 重要而又實用，意思是「弄清楚；搞明白」。數學不好的人（如我就是）常常背了公式卻不曉得箇中道理，苦啊。別緊張，以下不是數學，是英文練習：

小試身手

6. 我弄不清楚這個公式背後的理由。（公式：formula）

_____

（4）for one's benefit 為了某人好（4段）

The teacher knew my boss was blind, so when writing on the blackboard he would always explain a bit more clearly for his benefit.

老師知道他是瞎子，因此在黑板上寫的時候，一概特別為他講得比較清楚一點。

解析

benefit 最常見的意思為「利益；好處」，因此 for one's benefit 當然也就是「為了某人好」，「為某人設想、著想」的意思。

小試身手

7. 他們誤解我了。我這麼做真的是為了大家好。

_____

(5) give a（particularly）detailed description（特別）詳加解說（4段）

If the teacher drew a diagram on the board, he would have to give a particularly detailed description.

如果老師在黑板上劃了圖，更加要特別描述一番。

解析

在 give a（particularly）detailed description 裡，這個 give 的用法似乎只能意會，難以言傳。不過我們給你以下的練習幫你熟習：

小試身手

8. 為讓學生更加瞭解，老師接連舉了好幾個例子。

_____

(6) take a test(s) orally 考口試；口頭應試（5段）

When he took tests, he had to take them orally. He said every teacher would give him an individualized oral test.

考試只好用口試，他說每位老師都為他而舉行個別的口試。

解析

本句的學習目標在 take them（the tests）orally 和 individualized oral test。「考」試一般用 take 殆無疑義。可是考「口」試要怎麼說呢，你是否傷過腦筋呢？喔，原來是 take the tests orally，這個 orally 的重要性不言可喻。individualized oral test 是「個別口試」的意思。可能有讀者會有此一問：為什麼不是 individual 而是 individualized 呢？如果用的是 individual 可就變成「個人的；單獨的；一個一個來的」的意思了。但是在這裡則傾向是「個別量身定作的」之義，用 individual 不妥也不對。

小試身手

9. 關於考試，教授給兩個選擇：口試或紙筆測驗。

_____

(7) provide something for somebody 供應某物給某人
provide somebody with something 供應某人某物（6段）

In the US there's a nonprofit organization that provides recording services for the blind.

美國有一個盲人錄音服務社的非營利性組織。

解析

首先要介紹你認識 provide 的基本用法。常見的為 provide（某人）with（某物）和 provide（某物）for（某人）。所以你應不難理解譯文的寫法 provides recording services for the blind。那以下的句子要如何處理成英文呢？

小試身手

10. 我被供應所需的一切資源。

_____

(8) one's turn 輪到某人（6段）

There are incredibly many volunteers there, so many that most of them have to wait a long time before it's their turn to read a book.

義工奇多無比，大多數義工要等很久才輪到他念一本書。

解析

我們來看看 turn 的用法，通常它當動詞使用居多，如 He turned and left without saying a word. 但是在此處它卻是不折不扣的名詞，one's turn 作「輪到某人」解。

小試身手

11. 在你之後輪到誰呢？

_____

（9）in addition to... 除了……還有（6段）

Besides doing it out of love, the students had another reason to read...
除了出於愛心以外，還有一個原因。

解析

介紹一個片語 in addition to「除……以外（還加上……）」讓大家認識。因為是介詞，通常後面接名詞作受詞。如果後面緊跟著動詞時，這個不幸的動詞就只好淪為動名詞 Ving。它和介詞 besides 完全同義，完全相同的用法，也就是說，跟在 besides 之後的動詞也是 Ving。

小試身手

12. 除了出錢，他還出力。

_____

(10) ...(should, would, could, might)(not)have Vpp...(7段)

Otherwise, I don't think he could possibly have read so many books.
否則我想他不可能念到這麼多的書。

解析

這裡有個中國學生感到困難的觀念：與過去事實相反的假設。

以下有個過去事實：

他讀過許多書。He read many books.(read 此為過去式)

把以上的事實「顛倒過來」(讀→ 沒有讀)，句子就成了：

(因為種種理由，)他就無從讀那麼多書了。He could(not)have read so many books.(動詞用 could+ 完成式)

所以當需要表達過去本來可以(或者不可以)怎麼做的時候，得使用這個句構。請試著把這個句型和以上的英文句子作個對比，可以幫助你更容易體會其中奧妙。以下根據原來的故事情節另立一題，和原譯文有點淵源，但對中等程度的學習者仍有點難：

小試身手

13. 若沒有這些錄音服務，他就無從讀那麼多書了。

_____

(11) those who...(凡)⋯⋯的人(8段)

Those who understand computer science will be more curious to know how a blind man could write computer programs.
懂得計算機科學的人，一定更會好奇地想知道盲人如何寫計算機程式。

解析

those who...「（凡）……的人」可當句型看，和之前我們見過的句型 anyone who... 的用法和意義類似。兩者間的重大差別是 those who... 有 those 所以為複數形式，anyone who... 有 anyone 所以為單數形式。原譯文若用 anyone who... 來寫，則句子要寫成：Anyone who understands computer science will be... 你看出差別來了嗎？（因為是第三人稱單數，所以其後所接的現在式動詞為 understands）

小試身手

14. 我討厭不尊重他人的人。

_____

(12) the + adjective ……人（9段）

My boss studied thirty years ago, back when there was no computer equipment designed for the blind.

我老闆念書是三十年前的事，當時計算機沒有任何一樣替盲人著想的設備。

解析

英文有個用法，你不可不知。即定冠詞（the）後面隨著某些特定的形容詞可以表示「……的人」。所以 the blind 就相當於 blind people；the deaf 相當於 deaf people；the young 相當於 young people；the old 相當於 old people；而 the handicapped（disabled）就是 handicapped（disabled）people。

小試身手

15. 有才有德的人應為愚者服務。

_____

（13） **make a big fuss over...** 為……而大驚小怪（小題大作）（11段）

Society shouldn't discriminate against them, but it shouldn't make too big a fuss over them either.

社會不該歧視盲人，可是也不該對盲人過分地大驚小怪。

解析

make a big fuss over 是比較常用在日常生活中的口語，它的意思大抵是指把事情誇大渲染，喧騰吵鬧一番，相當於中文的為了某某事情而「大驚小怪」或「小題大作」。

小試身手

16. 他會為了無足輕重的小事而大鬧一番。

_____

（14） **Only**（子句／片語）……＋倒裝結構（11段）

Only after I interceded and my boss signed a document promising not to sue the airline **would they** finally **let** him on his flight.

最後還是由我出面，由老闆簽了一份文件，保證不會告某航空公司，某航空公司才肯讓他上機。

解析

英文有倒裝句構的現象，本句即是。讀者可以觀察到譯文裡粗體而劃底線的部分就是倒裝的部分。更具體而言，這些倒裝的結構大致如下：

助動詞 (would) ＋主詞 (they) ＋原形動詞 (let)……

不過我們要探究，好端端的句子為什麼要倒裝？往句子的前面再看去，Only after I interceded and my boss signed a document promising not to sue the airline 赫然在目。所以可以說，之所以產生倒裝，其實乃是 Only... 所造成的。

小試身手

17. 只有在下午三點到四點間他們才休息喝下午茶。

_____

---

(15) The moment... 一⋯⋯就⋯⋯（12段）

The moment they see anyone who's blind, they'll invite him to the VIP lounge...

他們一看到有盲人，會立刻請他到貴賓室去⋯⋯

解析

可曾想過 The moment... 也是個不可小覷的重點，它的意思為「一⋯⋯馬上就⋯⋯」。其實它還是個連接詞的作用，負責連接兩個子句，說明兩個子句動詞 (動作) 的時間前後相當靠近。

小試身手

18. 我一打開門，寵物狗就對我衝過來。

_____

---

(16) S+V+... without（someone）ever Ving... 而不待（某人）⋯⋯；⋯⋯而不需要（某人）⋯⋯（13段）

My boss says he's used about every means of transportation there is without ever asking anyone to pick him up. He's ridden trains, subways, etc. on his own without anyone ever refusing to let him on.

我老闆說他什麼交通工具都用過，從來沒有人接，火車、地下鐵等等他都一個人坐，從來沒有人拒絕他上去。

解析

without 本身即帶有否定之意，而 ever 常和否定意味的字詞合用，有加強否定的作用，有時候少了這個 ever 亦無不可。要注意的是，像這樣的結構常和前面的主結構相輔相成。即「某甲做了什麼事情而不待（而不需要）（某乙）……」。好像很複雜是嗎？其實並不會。自我挑戰一下就有心得了。

小試身手

19. Jack進到會議室，不待人請就找位子坐下。

_____

(17) think of 某人或某事 as... 把某人或某事當成……來看；將某人或某事視為……（14段）

We Chinese like to think of the blind as abject and pitiful.
我們中國人喜將盲人講得可憐兮兮的。

解析

這種句型本身的含意已經夠清楚了，而且在語法上也很貼近中文，並不難學。和它相近的有 see... as.../ view... as.../ regard... as.../ look upon... as... 等等。

小試身手

20. 他被當成民族英雄來看。

_____

(18) No wonder... 難怪……；無怪乎……（15段）

No wonder there are many blind foreigners who achieve outstanding academic success.

無怪乎盲洋人在學術上有傑出表現者多矣。

解析

這是一種接近慣用語法的句型，通常後面跟著子句，句意並不難理解，和它相似的慣用語有 Small wonder.../ Little wonder...。

小試身手

21. (發生事故了)難怪所有的列車都誤點。

_____

(19) get things mixed up 把……搞混在一起；把……弄得不清不楚（16段）

Actually, his mother didn't know much about math, so she probably got things mixed up a lot of the time.

其實他媽媽根本不懂數學，有時候大概都講錯了。

解析

mix 字面的意思為「混合；混摻」，所以 mixed up 當然就是「通通混在一起」或「亂七八糟」的意思。

小試身手

22. 既然我都搞不清楚，老師要我用用腦筋，把事情搞懂。（提示：「搞懂」用 straighten up）

_____

(20)（much）to one's surprise,... 令某人大為驚訝；令某人大感意外（17段）

...but instead, much to their surprise, he told all about his experiences playing poker with Chicago gangsters.

不料他大談和芝加哥黑道賭撲克的經驗。

解析

在這個結構裡，學習者要非常注意介詞 to，它的後面接著所有格（在原譯文裡為 their），之後再接著一個表示情緒的名詞。如果想加大、加深這種情緒，不妨考慮在介詞 to 之前添個 much 或者在該情緒名詞之前添個 great，以本句型而言就是：to one's（great）surprise,...

小試身手

23. 我的好友們都來參加我的慶生會，令我大為高興。（提示：delight）

＿＿＿＿＿＿＿＿＿＿＿＿＿＿＿＿＿＿＿＿＿＿＿＿＿

(21) fiercely loyal（friends）太講義氣的朋友（18段）

After my blind friend heard this, he no longer dared to associate with these guys who were so fiercely loyal to each other.

我的盲人朋友聽了以後，再也不敢和這些太講義氣的朋友來往了。

解析

此處非解釋句型，只是把它列出來，讓讀者欣賞妙譯。「講義氣」要譯成英文殊為不易，譯者以 fiercely loyal 輕鬆卻又傳神的把它譯出來。這裡講的是道上兄弟的義氣，fierce 有「兇猛」、「兇惡」之意，但是 fiercely 在此除了本身蘊含的意義，還多了一層「極為」、「非常」的意味。而 loyal 則是「忠誠」、「忠心耿耿」，兩者組合，用來詮釋江湖道上的「講義氣」，豈不令人拍案叫絕。我們不妨來個東施效顰。

24. 他對人很冷淡，即使是多年同事也不例外。(提示：coldly indifferent)

_____

(22) the handicapped(visually and hearing impaired)殘障人士；聽障和視障人士(19段)

I've come to realize that our entire society underestimates the ability of the handicapped.
我發現我們整個社會都低估了殘障者的能力。

Those in charge of the schools for the visually and hearing impaired that educate these children think the same way,...
我們負責這方面教育的啟聰啟明學校，也作如此想……

解析
要學會這個結構，一定不可輕忽定冠詞 the，這是它的一個很重要的用法。亦即 the handicapped 事實上就是 handicapped people；這麼說來，the visually and hearing impaired 不 就 是 visually and hearing impaired people 了嗎。值得注意的是，有時候這樣的結構它的意思是單數的意思，如 the accused(被告)；the deceased(死者)。還有，有些時候後面跟著一些純形容詞，例如：the young(= young people)/ the old(= old people)/ the sick(= sick people)/ the underprivileged(=underprivileged people)

25. 當你看到戰場的一切，有時候你會覺得死者比傷者幸運。

_____

（23）as long as... 只要……（20段）

As long as you have some trivial physical deficiency, you can't pursue a certain line of work.

只要一點點小小的身體上的缺陷，常常就不能進入某種職業。

解析

這個 as long as 我們是把它當成（從屬）連接詞來看的，和後面的一些字構成條件副詞子句，因為它和 if 在意思和用法上都非常接近。小時候唱兒歌，「哥哥爸爸真偉大……」，唱到最後不是「只要我長大」嗎？好，當下就試試看吧。

小試身手

26. 只要我長大，我就拿槍保衛國家。

_____

小試身手解答

1. Anyone who goes against him is severely punished.

2. He was bitter about the cold treatment he received.

3. He grabbed me by the arm.

4. I punched (hit, struck) him in the stomach.

5. Their love affair went on and off for six years.

6. I can't figure out the reasoning behind this math formula.

7. They misunderstood my intention. I did it truly for everyone's benefit.

8. To help the students understand more clearly, the teacher gave one example after another.

9. The professor offered two options for the test: oral or written.

10. I was provided with all the resources I needed.

11. Whose turn is it after yours?

12. In addition to (= Besides) donating money, he volunteers.

13. If there had been no such recording services, he could not have read so many books.

14. I detest those who do not respect others.

15. The talented should serve the foolish / less talented.

16. He tends to make a big fuss over trivial things.

17. Only between 3:00 pm and 4:00 pm did they have their tea break.

18. The moment I opened the door, my pet dog came rushing towards me.

19. Jack entered the conference room and took a seat without anyone (ever) asking him to.

20. He is looked upon (thought of) as a national hero.

21. (There was an accident.) Little wonder all the trains have been delayed.

22. Now that I've gotten things mixed up, the teacher wants me to use my brain to straighten them out.

23. To my great delight, all my good friends came to my birthday party.

24. He is coldly indifferent to people; even his colleagues of many years are no exception.

25. When you saw all this on the battlefield, you would sometimes feel that the dead were luckier than the wounded.

26. I'll pick up a rifle and protect our country as long as I grow up.

"My Mom Came to See Me"
—a true story

「我的媽媽來看我」
——一個真實的故事

1-5　　相信很多人都聽過一首童謠，歌詞中有一句話「我的媽媽拿著雨傘來接我」，這首童謠的意思好像是描寫一個幼稚園的小孩子，在幼稚園門口等媽媽來接他，正好碰到下雨，嚇得媽媽終於出現了，使這位小孩感到非常安心。

　　有一次，我在美國的一個購物中心買東西，忽然天色大變，強風夾著大雨，飛沙走石地橫掃而來，停車場中行人紛紛走避，而一對小孩卻在風雨中大哭地找尋他們的媽媽，我看風雨實在太大，把車門打開，暗示他們進入我的車內躲雨，小弟弟糊裡糊塗，就要進來，他的姐姐大概想到壞人騙小孩子的故事，一把將弟弟拖住，而且哭得更大聲，就在這時候，他們的媽媽及時出現了，孩子們看到媽媽以後的歡樂表情，使我終生難忘。

　　孩子們在風雨中等待媽媽，大家可以想像得到，我卻要在這裡講一個成人在困境中想念媽媽的故事，其實這不是故事，這是我親身經歷的事實。

CD1-8
◇ nursery song (n.) 兒歌；童謠
◇ lyrics (n.) 歌詞
◇ relieved (adj.) 如釋重負的；鬆了一口氣的
◇ mingle (v.) 摻雜；混在一起

I bet a lot of people have heard a nursery song that contains the lyrics, "My mom came to pick me up with an umbrella in her hand." This song seems to be about a child who is waiting at the entrance of his kindergarten for his mom to pick him up when it begins to rain. Fortunately, his mother eventually appears, and the little boy feels very relieved.

One time, I was shopping at a mall in America when there was a sudden drastic change in the sky. Pouring rain mingled with strong wind swept toward us, flinging sand and rocks. The pedestrians in the parking lot fled in confusion, but a pair of children caught in the wind and rain sobbed as they looked for their mom. I saw how big the storm was, so I opened my car door and signaled for them to take shelter from the rain inside my car. The little brother, who didn't know any better, was about to come in when his big sister, who probably remembered stories about bad people tricking children, grabbed her brother and held him back, then cried even louder. Right at that moment, their mother appeared. I will never forget the expressions of joy that appeared on the children's faces when they saw their mom.

Anyone can imagine children waiting for their mother in the rain, but the story I have to tell is of a grown man in dire straits who missed his mother. Actually, this isn't just a mere story— this is a real experience that I myself went through.

◇ pedestrian (n.) 路人；行人
◇ trick (v.) 哄騙
◇ expression (n.) (臉部) 表情
◇ dire (adj.) 悲慘的；危殆的

三十年前，我在大學念書，我常常去台北監獄探訪受刑人，我還記得那時候，台北監獄在愛國西路，我們的辦法是和受刑人打打籃球，同時也和一些人聊聊天。

當時，有一位黝黑瘦高的受刑人似乎最和我談得來，他很喜歡看書，因此我就設法送了很多的書給他看，我發現在眾多的受刑人中間，他所受的教育比較高，他是台北市一所有名中學畢業的，比我大七、八歲。受刑人每星期大概可以有三次見客，我去看別的都會吃閉門羹。可是這位受刑人，永遠可以見我，至少我從未吃過閉門羹。

6-10　他常在我面前提起他媽媽，說他媽媽是位非常慈祥的女性，他說他媽媽常常來看他，可是我始終不太相信這一點。

這位受刑人當時所住的地方其實是看守所，沒有定罪的受刑人都關在這裡，審判終結的人才再換到其他監獄去。我的這位朋友有一天告訴我，他要搬家了，因為他已被定罪，要正式服刑了。我這才發現他有軍人身分，大概是在服兵役時犯的罪，所以要到新店的軍人監獄去服刑。

◇ undergraduate (n.) 大學部學生　　◇ swarthy (adj.) 黝黑的
◇ inmate (n.) 囚犯　　◇ detention (n.) 拘留；羈押

Thirty years ago, when I was an undergraduate, I'd often go to the Taipei prison to visit the inmates there. I still remember that back then the Taipei jail was on Aiguo West Road. We'd usually just shoot hoops with the prisoners or chat with a few of them.

At that time, there was a swarthy, tall and skinny inmate who seemed to get along with me best. He loved to read, so I'd find ways to bring him lots of books. I discovered that among all the inmates, he was the best educated. He had graduated from a famous Taipei high school and was seven or eight years older than me. The prisoners were allowed to see visitors roughly three times a week. Whenever I went to see the other prisoners, they would close their doors and refuse to see me. This one, however, could always meet with me, or at any rate, he never shut the door in my face.

When he was with me, he often mentioned his mom, saying what a kind-hearted woman she was. He said she often came to see him, but I always had my doubts about that.

6-10

The place where this prisoner lived then was actually a detention house. All the prisoners who hadn't yet been convicted were kept there; only those whose trials had finished were transferred to other jails. One day this friend of mine told me he was moving away because he had been convicted and was to begin formally serving his sentence. Only then did I discover that he had been a soldier. Most likely he had committed a crime while in the service; that was why he was to go to the Xindian military prison to serve his time.

◇ convict(v.)定罪；定讞　　◇ transfer(v.)移送　　　◇ commit(v.)犯(罪)

　　當他到新店的軍人監獄去服刑時，我也成了預備軍官，我在台北服役，週末有時會去看他，我記得要去新店的軍人監獄，要經過空軍公墓。再經過一條大樹成蔭的路，軍人監獄就在這條路的盡頭。

　　有一次我去看他，發現他被禁止接見，我和警衛打打交道，發現大概一個多月以後才可以看到我的朋友。一個月以後，我終於看到他了，這次他告訴我一個很可憐的故事。他說他在服刑期間做工，也賺了一些錢，我記得那個數字實在少得可憐，可是這是他全部的積蓄，因此他一直偷偷地把這幾十塊錢放在一個很秘密的地方，沒有想到他的某位長官把他的錢偷掉了，我的朋友一氣之下和他的這位長官大打出手。

　　各位可以想像我的朋友的悲慘遭遇，他這種犯上的事情是相當嚴重的，他被人在晚上拖到廣場去痛打一頓，事後他被關在一間小的牢房裡，而且二十四小時地戴上手銬。

11-15　　我的朋友告訴我這些事情時留下了眼淚，我們談話的時候，旁邊總有一個身強體壯的兵在旁聽，說到這些事，我記得那個兵面無表情地看著遠處，假裝沒有聽到。

◇ armed forces 武裝軍力；軍隊
◇ reserve officer 預官
◇ forbid (v.) 禁止

◇ stash (v.) 收；藏匿
◇ caution (n.) 小心；謹慎
◇ handcuffs (n.) 手銬

When he went to the Xindian military prison to begin his sentence, I also entered the armed forces as a reserve officer. I served in Taipei, and occasionally I'd go see him on the weekend. I recall that to get to the Xindian military prison, you had to go through the air force cemetery, then along a street shaded by big trees, at the end of which was the prison.

Once when I went to see him, I discovered that he had been forbidden to see visitors. By striking up a conversation with a guard, I found out I'd have to wait for over a month to see my friend again. A month later, I finally saw him, and he told me a very sad story. He said he had earned some money by working during his sentence. I remember the amount was pitifully small, but it was all his savings, so he always furtively stashed those few dollars in a secret place. In spite of his caution, though, one of his officers stole all his money. In a fit of anger, he got into a big fistfight with the officer.

You can imagine the tragic result that followed for my friend. This sort of attack on authority was viewed extremely seriously. At night he was dragged to the yard and beaten severely, then locked away in a tiny cell where he had to wear handcuffs 24 hours a day.

My friend shed tears as he told me these things. During our entire conversation, there was a big, burly soldier by our side listening to what we said. When we got to this point in the conversation, I recall that the soldier looked away expressionlessly, pretending he hadn't heard what we said.

◇ recall (v.) 回憶；回想　　　　　◇ pretend (v.) 佯裝；假裝

　　忽然我的朋友又提到他媽媽了，他說你如果看到我的媽媽，一定會比較看得起我，他說他常常感到萬念俱灰，可是一想到媽媽，他心情又會比較好一點。

　　既然他一再提起他媽媽，我就問了他家地址，然後我在一個星期六的黃昏，騎了我的老爺腳踏車，到他家去看他的媽媽。

　　他的家在現在的忠孝東路，在當時，那條路叫做中正路，我發現他的家好遠，快到松山了。房子是典型的日式房子，附近每一棟都一樣，顯然是中低層公務員宿舍。我穿了全套的空軍少尉制服，很有禮貌的介紹我自己，也報上我朋友的名字。

　　這家人好像有幾位比我還年輕的小孩，我被安頓在他們大約兩三坪大的客廳裡坐下，我記得這個客廳裡布置得極為簡陋，只有幾把破舊的椅子，我坐下以後，發現氣氛有點不自然，而我很快地明瞭這是怎麼一回事了。

◇ despair (n.) 絕望；灰心失意
◇ improve (v.) 好轉；變好
◇ ancient (adj.) 古早的；古老的
◇ dormitory (n.) 宿舍
◇ civil servant (n.) 公務員；公僕
◇ courteously (adv.) 客氣地；有禮地

Suddenly my friend mentioned his mom again. He said, if you saw my mom, you'd surely think better of me. He said he often felt great discouragement and despair, but as soon as he thought of his mother, his mood would improve a little.

Seeing how he repeatedly mentioned his mother, I asked for his family's address. Then, one Saturday evening, I rode my ancient bicycle to his house to see his mom.

His house was where Zhongxiao East Road is today; back then it was called Zhongzheng Road. I discovered his house was quite a fair distance away, almost all the way to Songshan. It was a classic Japanese-style house. Every building in the neighborhood was the same; they were clearly dormitories for mid- to lower-level civil servants. Wearing my full air force lieutenant's uniform, I introduced myself very courteously and mentioned my friend's name.

This family seemed to have a few children younger than me. I was ushered into their living room, which was only two or three *ping* in size, to sit down. This living room, as I recall, was very sparsely and crudely furnished: there were only a few worn-out chairs. After I sat down, I realized the atmosphere felt rather unnatural, and it didn't take me long to figure out why.

◇ sparsely (adv.) 稀疏地
◇ crudely (adv.) 簡陋地

◇ furnish (v.) 陳設；布置（指房子內部桌椅櫥櫃家具及廚房設施等）

16-20　　　我朋友的爸爸進來了，他們父子很相像，他非常嚴肅地告訴我，他早已不承認這個不爭氣的兒子，因為他簡直不能相信他們家會有這種丟臉的兒子，所以不僅早已不和他兒子來往，而且也一直禁止家人和他來往。自從他進入了監獄，他們全家沒有一個人和他來往過。

　　　我立刻想起，怪不得我一直可以見到我的好朋友，原來他的媽媽事實上從來沒有去看過他，他說「我的媽媽來看我」，只是他的一種幻想而已。

　　　我也看到了他的媽媽，他的媽媽是個典型的中國婦女，瘦瘦的，個子相當矮，衣著非常樸素，她始終沒有講一句話。

　　　我卻不管他爸爸怎麼講，一五一十地告訴他們全家人，我的朋友是非常想念他的媽媽。可是這位嚴厲的爸爸卻暗示我該滾蛋了，我想虧得我穿上空軍制服，而且自我介紹過我是台大電機系畢業的，否則我早就被趕出去了。

◇ disown (v.) 斷絕關係
◇ correspond (v.) 書信來往；通訊；通郵
◇ fantasy (n.) 空想；胡思亂想
◇ plainly (adv.) 簡單樸素地

16-20

My friend's father entered; the two of them looked very much alike. He told me very sternly that he had disowned this good-for-nothing boy of his long ago because he simply couldn't believe his family would have such a disgrace for a son. Thus, not only had he not spoken with his son for a long time, but he had forbidden the rest of the family from corresponding with him as well. Ever since he had gone to jail, not once had a single member of their family ever been in touch with him.

A thought immediately occurred to me: no wonder I was always able to see my good friend— his mother had never actually come to see him at all! When he said, "My mom came to see me," it was nothing more than a fantasy.

I also saw his mother, a stereotypical Chinese woman: slim, rather short and very plainly dressed. She never spoke a word the entire time.

Despite what his father had said, though, I proceeded to candidly tell the whole family how my friend really missed his mom. But the stern father hinted that I'd better be on my way. It's a good thing I wore my air force uniform and mentioned when I introduced myself that I had a BS in Electrical Engineering from NTU; otherwise I think I would have been kicked out long before.

◇ proceed(v.)開始；進行
◇ BS 理學士學位(Bachelor of Science)

◇ NTU 國立台灣大學(National Taiwan University)

　　我以非常失望的心情離開他的家，他的爸爸在門口還提醒我以後不必再來了。

21-25　　可是我的腳踏車才一轉彎，我就聽到了後面的腳步聲，他的一個妹妹匆匆趕來，叫住了我，他的媽媽跟在後面，她要知道如何能找到她兒子，因為她要去看他。我趕快告訴他們如何到新店軍人監獄，她們以最快的速度謝了我，馬上趕回家去。

　　當時天色已黑，我所在地方是個很冷清而且幾乎有點荒涼的地方，四週都是一些木造的日式房子，每棟房子都有一個用竹籬笆圍起來的小院子，現在每戶人家都點上了燈，我可以感到家家親人團聚的溫暖，我知道我的朋友和他母親即將真的見面，我真的感到在冥冥之中一定有一個上蒼在安排一切，而我正是祂所選的一個工具。

　　果真，我不能去看我的朋友了，他從監獄中寫了一封信給我，告訴我他和他母親見面了。而我開始辦理退伍手續，準備去美國念書，臨走以前，我又和他見了最後一面。這次他胖了，也有了笑容，他說他媽媽常帶菜給他，所以他胖了一點，他也告訴我家裡弟弟妹妹考各級學校的情形。最後他問我退伍以後要做什麼，我說我要去美國念書，忽然之間，他的笑容消失了，他說：「你相不相信？我真的感謝你這

◇ desolate（adj.）冷清的；荒涼的　　　　◇ invisible（adj.）看不見的

I left his house extremely disappointed. At the doorway, his dad reminded me that there was no need for me to come again in the future.

But my bike had only just turned the corner when I heard footsteps behind me. One of his younger sisters rushed toward me and called for me to stop, and his mother followed behind. She wanted to know how to find her son, because she wanted to go see him. I hurriedly told them how to get to the military prison in Xindian. They thanked me as fast as they could and then immediately rushed back home.

21-25

The sky was already black then, and I found myself in a quiet, almost desolate, place. All around me were wooden Japanese-style houses, each one with a little yard surrounded by a bamboo fence. The people in every house all had their lights turned on. I could feel the warmth of house after house full of loved ones gathered together. I knew my friend and his mother would soon meet for real. I felt certain that there was an invisible but very real God arranging everything, and I was an instrument He had chosen.

CD1-7

Just as I had expected, I couldn't go see my friend anymore after that. He wrote me a letter from jail telling me that he had seen his mother face to face. Meanwhile, I started taking care of my military discharge procedures and preparing to go study in the US. Just before I left, I met with him for the last time. He had gotten fatter, and he wore a smile. He said his mom often came to bring him food, so he'd

◇ instrument(n.)工具(註：在這裡指的是「讓事情工作能順利完成的人或物」，即冥冥中上帝有所安排，特別挑選他來促成母子相會這件事)
◇ procedure(n.)手續；程序

些日子來看我，也使我和我家人團圓，遺憾的是我們兩人之間的友誼會從此完了，因為你將來可以在社會上一步一步地爬上去，而我卻是一個犯人，我們之間的距離會越來越大，我們不可能再繼續做朋友的。」

　　他又接著說：「你有沒有考慮過？索性專門留下來，終身為我們這種人服務？」

　　我默然無語，我的虛榮心使我不肯放棄追逐名利的機會，三十年過去了，我始終為我未能終身為受刑人服務慚愧不已，每次我在事業上有所成就，反而使我感到良心不安。我在此謝謝我的這位朋友，他使我感到我這一生沒有白過，我現在至少可以驕傲地告訴我的女兒「你的爸爸曾經做過好事」，我已五十多歲，我的朋友恐怕已是六十歲，希望他能知道，他對我講的話對我影響相當之大，我之所以決定離開美國，回來服務，也多多少少因為他說「你有沒有考慮過留下來？」這句話。

◇ social ladder 社會階梯。由基層往高　◇ speechless(adj.)無言的
　處爬，如爬梯子一般　　　　　　　　◇ pursue(v.)追求；追逐
◇ criminal(n.)罪犯　　　　　　　　　◇ conscience(n.)良知；良心

put on a little weight. He also told me how his little brothers and sisters were doing in their exams at school. Finally, he asked me what I was going to do after getting out of the air force. I told him I was going to America to study. All of his sudden his smile disappeared, and he said, "Can you believe it? I'm really thankful to you for coming to see me all this time and for reuniting me with my family. It's just too bad that our friendship will be over after this. You'll climb up the social ladder step by step, but I'm only a criminal; the distance between us will get greater and greater, and we can't keep being friends."

He continued, "Have you ever considered, well, just... just staying here and spending your whole life helping people like me?"

I was speechless. My vanity made me unwilling to give up the opportunity to pursue fame and wealth. Thirty years have passed since then, but the deep shame of being unable to dedicate my life to serving prisoners has never left me. Every time I have success in my career, it only puts my conscience ill at ease. Here I'd like to take the opportunity to thank this friend of mine for making me feel I haven't lived my life in vain. At least now I can proudly tell my daughter, "Your dad once did a good thing." I'm now in my fifties, and I'm afraid my friend is now sixty. I hope he can know how much what he said has influenced me. My decision to leave the US and return to serve Taiwan was due in no small degree to his words: "Have you ever considered staying here?"

◇　vain(adj.)沒有意義的；沒有價值的(註：原英譯...I haven't lived my life in vain 相當
於中文「我沒有虛度此生」)

26-27　　世界上有很多職業，要做得非常好，才對社會上有影響，我常想，一個平庸的舞蹈家就搞不出所以然來，可是做母親，就不同了，即使做一個平凡的母親，一樣可以對社會有非常正面的影響。

　　我希望有一根魔棒，一揮之下，天下的母親都是平凡而慈祥的好母親，我相信我們的監獄會因此空了一半，我再揮一下這支魔棒，我國有幾萬個義工肯替監獄裡的受刑人服務，我相信我們的監獄會更加再空了一半。

26-27

There are many jobs in the world that you have to do extremely well in order to influence society. I often think, a mediocre dancer won't make much of an impact in the world, but being a mother is different— even if you're just an ordinary mother, you can still have an extremely positive influence on society.

I wish I had a magic wand that I could wave once to make all the world's mothers ordinary, kind-hearted, good mothers. I believe that our jails would be emptied by half as a result. If I could wave the wand again and make my country have tens of thousands of volunteers willing to serve the prisoners in the jails, I believe our prisons would be emptied by half yet again.

◇ mediocre [`midɪˌokɚ] (adj.) 中等的；平庸的

◇ positive (adj.) 正面的；肯定的；積極的

◇ magic wand 魔杖（即魔術師在表演戲法時手上所拿的細長棒子）

（1）**feel relieved**（agitated, discouraged, disheartened, humiliated, baffled, ...）（1段）

Fortunately, his mother eventually appears, and the little boy feels very relieved.

虧得媽媽終於出現了，使這位小孩感到非常安心。

解析

處理事情、和人相處，不免心理會有些感覺或感觸，在中文裡，我們常說（某人）覺得（悲哀、欣喜、沮喪、得意、忿怒、失望……），而英文就以 feel（grieved, delighted, frustrated, elated, infuriated, disappointed,...），請注意動詞 feel 後面所接的都是已經形容詞化的 Vpp（過去分詞）。

> **小試身手**
>
> 1. 他所提出的可笑藉口讓我覺得越來越火大。
>
> _____

（2）**be caught in the rain**（storm, heat, typhoon,...）無法自……脫身（脫困）（2段）

The pedestrians in the parking lot fled in confusion, but a pair of children caught in the wind and rain sobbed as they looked for their mom.

停車場中行人紛紛走避，而一對小孩卻在風雨中大哭地找尋他們的媽媽。

解析

catch 的本意為「抓住」，被動形式 be caught 當然就是「被抓住」，引申後的結果就是「被牢牢抓住無法脫困」。在溪流中戲水，被暗流捲住，無法脫困，就可以用 be caught in the undercurrent 來表示。有人設計陷害你，讓

你坐困愁城，難脫困局，可以用 be caught in the trick (setup) 來表示。

小試身手

2.　我發現自己被四面而來的濃霧困住。

_____

（3）not know any better 不知情；不懂事；不明就裡（2段）

The little brother, who didn't know any better, was about to come inside my car.

小弟弟糊裡糊塗，就要進來。

解析

這種獨特的英語表達方式對學習者來說真是有點頭痛。我們就這麼講好了，你的好朋友數學考不及格，告訴你他的成績是 15 分，然後他反問你考了幾分，你的成績是 13 分，這時你可用 I didn't do any better. 這句話回敬他，意思就是說「我也好不到哪裡去」或「我考得一樣爛」。所以句型裡的 not know any better 基本上就是「所知也沒多到哪裡去」或「不明就裡」的意思。

小試身手

3.　我們找個路人問路，他似乎也搞不清楚火車站在哪兒。

_____

（4）shoot hoops 打籃球；投籃（4段）

We'd usually just shoot hoops with the prisoners or chat with a few of them.

我們的辦法是和受刑人打打籃球，同時也和一些人聊聊天。

解析

很生活化的口語英文，看到這句話，再想想在學校正統英文課所學的 play basketball，你會覺得這樣子的口語英文活潑生動多了。不過這也是異地學英文的難處，不是生活在當地英語環境裡，很難學到這種英文的。話說回來，shoot 在這裡是「投射」的意思，而 hoop 指的是「籃框」，兩者相加，意思其實也很明顯了。順便一提，打籃球時，有人一記三分遠射，漂亮空心中的，你可以誇他一句 (A)Nice shot.

小試身手

4. 他在公園裡的球場和朋友打籃球。

_____

（5）get along with... 與……有交情；與……相處融洽（5段）

At that time, there was a swarthy, tall and skinny inmate who seemed to get along with me best.

當時，有一位黝黑瘦高的受刑人似乎最和我談得來。

解析

這個片語大概頗令學習者費解，get along 表示相處得來，雙方沒有扞格不合的地方，along 本身即帶有「順著」、「沿著」的意味，有時再加上 well 這個字，變成 get along well with，則「相處和睦」的意思就更加清楚了。

小試身手

5. 聽說他沒什麼社交技巧。他根本不懂如何和人相處。

_____

(6) Only（副詞，副詞子句）＋倒裝結構（7段）

Only then did I discover that he was a soldier.

我這才發現他有軍人身分。

解析

這是個簡單卻重要的文法觀念：only 之後隨著副詞、副詞片語、副詞子句（大抵為表時間和地方的副詞），而且位置在句首時，之後的句子要以倒裝的結構呈現。

小試身手

6. 要被帶到他面前時，我才明白我犯的錯誤有多嚴重。

_____

(7) pitifully small（little, low,...）（小；少；低）得可憐（9段）

I remember the amount was pitifully small, but it was all his savings...

我記得那個數字實在少得可憐，可是這是他全部的積蓄……

解析

讀者不妨冷靜思考，當我們使用中文，説出「少得可憐」時，重點在哪裡呢？當然重點在「少」這個字，因為「可憐」是在説明「少」的程度，「少（little）」是形容詞，那麼「可憐」修飾「少」，當然用的是副詞（pitifully）的

形式。

小試身手

7. 他們有個共同點。(他們)都是出身家境非常清寒的家庭。

_____

---

(8) think better of somebody：更加看重(某人)；更加看得起 (某人)(12段)

He said, "If you saw my mom, you'd think better of me."
他說你如果看到我的媽媽，一定會比較看得起我。

解析

不少讀者應該都學過 speak well of...(誇獎讚美某人)speak ill of ...(詆毀中傷某人)。由此讀者不難體會 think much of... 和 think little of... 這兩個片語的意思了。

小試身手

8. 在他優異的表現之後，人們對他另眼相看(更看得起他)。

_____

---

(9) 地方副詞子句：where S. + V. + ...(14段)

His house was where Zhongxiao East Road is today...
他的家在現在的忠孝東路……

解析

地方副詞可以是單字 (home, abroad, upstairs, inside, everywhere...)，可

以是片語 (on the kitchen counter, in the bag, over the bridge...)，可以是子句 (where I work)，子句的彈性較小，幾乎就是以 where... 開頭。要注意的是時式，他（當時的）家 (His house **was**) 是在現在的忠孝東路 (where Zhongxiao East Road **is** today)，動詞一個使用過去式 was，一個使用現在式 is。

小試身手

9.　她走到窗邊，坐在她母親以前縫紉的地方。

　　_____

---

(10) **not once** 倒裝結構……(16段)

Ever since he went to jail, not once had a single member of their family ever been in touch with him.

自從他進入了監獄，他們全家沒有一個人和他來往過。

解析

not once 的意思為「沒有一次」、「一次都沒有」，是個否定副詞，基本上這類東西放到句首時，會影響到後面句子的順序，在原譯文裡就是過去完成式 (...had ever been...) 裡的助動詞 (had) 被拿到主詞前面去了。也就是說，原來的句子應該是：

... not a single member of their family had ever been in touch with him once.

把 not 和 once 一起拿到句首，然後再把助動詞 (had) 與主詞 (a single member of their family) 倒裝，結果就是：

... not once had (a single member of their family) ever been in touch with him.

小試身手

10. 我絕不向他借錢。（提示：用 under no circumstances 和倒裝結構。）

_____

（11）It's a good thing（that）... 幸好……；還好……（19段）

It's a good thing I wore my air force uniform and mentioned when I introduced myself...

虧得我穿上空軍制服，而且自我介紹過我是……

解析

中文有個講話的習慣「還好……」、「幸好……」、「多虧……」而英文就是 It's a good thing（that）...，中英文在表達這方面的意思倒是很相近，不算難學。

小試身手

11. 還好我戴了安全帽，否則我不敢想像會受到什麼傷害。

_____

（12）as... as somebody can（could）……（21段）

They thanked me as fast as they could and then immediately rushed back home.

她們以最快的速度謝了我，馬上趕回家去。

解析

類似 as... as one can（could）的結構在文法上稱之為「程度副詞子句」，修飾

前面的動詞（在原句中為 thank），描述感謝對方時的樣子。

小試身手

12. 我用溫和的不能再溫和的口吻和她說話，希望她能看清事實。

---

(13) take care of... the procedures... 處理……；著手進行…… (23段)

And I started taking care of my military discharge procedures and preparing to go study in the US.

我開始辦理退伍手續，準備去美國念書。

解析

take care of 在這裡是「料理」、「處理」的意思，和常見的「照顧」、「照料」不太一樣。中文「手續」用 procedures 來表達也很恰當。

小試身手

13. 因為少了一些身分文件，我在手續進行到一半時卡住了。

（14）dedicate one's life to... 一輩子奉獻……（25段）

Thirty years have passed since then, but the deep shame of being unable to dedicate my life to serving prisoners has never left me.

三十年過去了，我始終為我未能終身為受刑人服務慚愧不已。

解析

dedicate 的本意是「奉獻」而 to 的基本意義是「給」，兩者放在一起，意思算相當清楚，另外動詞可改用 devote 替代，意思差不多。要特別注意 to 在這個片語裡是介詞，後面所跟的動詞要用動名詞形式 Ving。

小試身手

14. 付出好幾個月的努力，他們讓那個計劃非常成功。

＿＿＿＿＿＿＿＿＿＿＿＿＿＿＿＿＿＿＿＿＿＿

（15）put one's conscience ill at ease... 令某人良心難安（25段）

Every time I have success in my career, it only puts my conscience ill at ease.

每次我在事業上有所成就，反而使我感到良心不安。

解析

at ease 本身是「安適」、「坦然」的意思，那麼 ill at ease 當然就是「不安適」、「不坦然」的意思了。

小試身手

15. 看到他就坐在桌子對面讓我覺得很彆扭。

＿＿＿＿＿＿＿＿＿＿＿＿＿＿＿＿＿＿＿＿＿＿

(16) I wish (that) 假設語氣 我願……(27段)

I wish I had a magic wand...

我希望有一根魔棒……

解析

我們常對於做不到的事抱著一個願望，明明知道百分百不可能，放在心裡想想，望梅止渴一番，也可以得到個幾分慰藉。譬如，在炎炎夏日時，你在心裡想著「真巴不得是個冬日」；在讀教科書時，心裡邊咒罵邊想著，「真希望手上拿著的是漫畫書」。這種根本和事實背道而馳的胡思亂想，用英文表達可得使用假設語氣。而假設語氣之難就在於它所用的動詞和我們平常使用的動詞不同，就拿以上「真巴不得是個冬日」和「真希望手上拿著的是漫畫書」兩句話來說，它們的情況是與現在事實相反（現在怎麼會是冬日呢？）（手上拿的怎麼會是漫畫呢？）這時候，英文句子就得使用過去式動詞來表達出這句話的內容是假的。好了，如果你讀這本書的當下是炎炎夏日，就拿以下這句來練習。（如果是個蕭瑟的冬天，就把冬日改成夏日就得了。）

小試身手

16. 真巴不得是個冬日。

_____

小試身手解答

1. I was getting more and more agitated over the ridiculous excuses he presented.

2. I found myself caught in a heavy fog rolling in from every direction.

3. We asked a pedestrian and he didn't seem to know any better where the railroad station is.

4. He's shooting hoops with his buddies on the court in the park.

5. They say he doesn't have any social skills. He just doesn't know how to get along with people.

6. Only when I was brought into his presence did I realize how serious a mistake I had made.

7. They have something in common: they all come from homes with pitifully low incomes.

8. People thought better of him after his excellent performance.

9. She walked up to the window and sat where her mother used to do her sewing.

10. Under no circumstances will I borrow money from him.

11. It's a good thing I wore my crash helmet; otherwise, I wouldn't dare to imagine what serious injury I might have suffered.

12. I talked to her in as soft a tone as I could, hoping to bring her back to

reality.

13. I got stuck midway through the procedures for lack of some ID papers.

14. They dedicated months and months of effort to the project, making it a great success.

15. The sight of him sitting across the table makes me feel ill at ease.

16. I wish(How I wish)it were a winter day.

Journey to the Moorland
荒原之旅

1-5　　當我告訴一位英國友人我要去蘇格蘭的蒼穹島的時候，這位英國人用指頭封住自己的嘴，輕輕地說：「噓，千萬不要讓別人知道你要去蒼穹島，我們絕不能讓大批旅客湧入哪裡，尤其不能讓庸俗的美國人知道這個島。」

　　到英國去看荒原，似乎是個荒唐的主意。

　　很多英國的小說中，常常會提到荒原，《咆哮山莊》是個最好的例子，男女主角常常在荒原中見面，書中也一再地描寫咆哮山莊附近的荒涼景色，《簡愛》是另一個例子，男主角眼睛瞎了以後，仍然對著荒原呼叫女主角的名字。即使福爾摩斯的偵探小說裡，很多故事也都發生在荒原裡，我們常常看到福爾摩斯來到一個鄉下的巨宅，晚上從臥室的窗中，可以看到濃霧正在慢慢地籠罩著外面的荒原，就在這個荒原裡，有人在策劃一個可怕的謀殺案。

　　英國的荒原當然不是什麼世界的名山大川，可是它最大的好處，是荒原仍然是荒原，對於我這種想逃離文明世界的人而言，英國的荒原仍然有無比的吸引力。

CD1-13

◇ overrun (v.) 橫行肆虐

◇ vulgar [ˋvʌlgɚ] (adj.) 粗野的；沒有教養的；沒有氣質的

◇ excellent (adj.) 絕佳的；上好的

◇ protagonist [proˋtæɡənɪst] (n.) (電影；戲劇；故事；小說) 主角

◇ character (n.) (電影；戲劇；故事；小說) 角色

When I told a British friend I was going to the Isle of Skye in Scotland, he held his finger to his mouth and whispered, "Shh! Be sure not to let anyone else know you're going to Skye. We mustn't let a crowd of tourists overrun the place. We especially mustn't let the vulgar Americans know about the island."

1-5
CD1-9

It seems like a crazy idea, going to Britain to see the moorland.

Lots of English novels often mention moorland; *Wuthering Heights* is an excellent example. The male and female protagonists often meet on the moor, and the book also contains multiple descriptions of the wild scenery around Wuthering Heights. *Jane Eyre* is another example. After the main male character goes blind, he still calls out the heroine's name to the moorland. Even in Sherlock Holmes detective novels, many of the stories are set in the moorland. We often read of Holmes going to a mansion out in the country, where from the bedroom window at night he can see thick fog slowly enshrouding the wilderness outdoors, the very wilderness where someone is plotting a frightful murder.

Of course, the moorland in Britain has no world-renowned wilderness or mighty rivers. But its greatest advantage is that it's still wilderness. To someone like me who wants to escape from the civilized world, the British moorland still holds a very powerful allure.

◇ heroine [ˈhɛroˌɪn] (n.) (電影；戲劇；故事；小說) 女主角
◇ enshroud (v.) 籠罩
◇ world-renowned (adj.) 世界知名的；大名頂頂的；馳譽世界的
◇ civilized (adj.) 文明的；開化的
◇ allure (n.) 魅力；吸引；誘惑

只有五天的假期，我只好選了兩個荒原，一個是蘇格蘭西海岸的蒼穹島，一個是勃朗特姐妹（《咆哮山莊》和《簡愛》的作者）住過的哈華斯荒原。

6-10　　到蒼穹島，大多數人都先到蘇格蘭最北的大城，印威內斯。我在晚上十點鐘左右才到印威內斯，找到了一家小旅館，旅館老闆一看就是那種蘇格蘭土生土長的人，紅圓的臉，一團和氣，他領我去一間閣樓似的房間，唯一的窗是一個天窗，可以看到外面的滿天星斗，旅館老闆說這旅館其實從前是他的家，他小時候就睡在這間房，他說可惜今晚不下雨，否則你可以聽到雨滴灑在屋頂和天窗的聲音，極有詩意。

　　到蒼穹島的火車一早六時四十五分離開，車廂裡只有兩個人，我和一位從澳洲來的化學教授，這位化學教授一定是個性情中人，他告訴我曾經專程從哥拉斯哥坐火車向西行，坐到盡頭以後再乘原車回去，他說他那次火車之旅，是在冬天，火車外都是蓋著雪的山和荒原，途

◇ ruddy（adj.）（臉色）紅潤的
◇ born-and-bred（adj.）土生土長的；生於斯長於斯的（註：英譯 a truly born-and bred Scot 就相當於中文的「一位不折不扣的蘇格蘭人」、「一位貨真價實的蘇格蘭人」）

Since I only had a five-day vacation, the best I could do was to choose two moorlands. One was the Isle of Skye, off the western coast of Scotland; the other was the Haworth moorland, where the Brontë sisters (the authors of *Wuthering Heights* and *Jane Eyre*) had once lived.

6-10

To get to the Isle of Skye, most people first go to Scotland's northernmost big city, Inverness. It was ten o'clock at night when I finally arrived in Inverness. I found a little inn where I could tell at first sight that the innkeeper, with his ruddy, round face and friendly manner, was a true born-and-bred Scot. He led me to a room that rather resembled an attic. The only window was in the ceiling; you could see the sky full of stars outside. The innkeeper said this inn was in fact his former home. When he was little, he slept in this room. He said, it was a pity it wasn't raining that night; otherwise I could hear the raindrops falling on the roof and skylight. The sound, he said, was very poetic.

The train to Skye left in the early morning at six forty-five. There were only two people in our compartment: myself and a chemistry professor from Australia, a genuine, forthright man. He told me he had once taken a special train trip from Glasgow westward to the end of the track, then back along the same line. That trip, he said, was in the winter: the scenery outside the train was all mountains and wild plains blanketed in snow. Along the way, lakes so clear you could see

◇ resemble (v.) (外貌長相) 相像；酷似
◇ former (adj.) 之前的；以前的
◇ skylight (n.) (屋頂的) 天窗
◇ genuine (adj.) 真正的；純正的
◇ blanket (v.) 完全覆蓋

中常有清澈見底的湖出現，將這些山倒映在湖邊，夕陽西下時，美到了極點。

我們的火車，在大霧中離開了印威內斯城，依依稀稀地可以看到翠綠的牧場，雖然有霧，已經有人騎馬在原野中慢行。火車先往北開，因此在東方也正好在大霧上面升起了紅紅的太陽，草原、樹叢、低頭吃草的牛羊，這種景色連續了一個小時之久。

印威內斯是個相當不錯的城市，附近原野稱不上什麼荒原，應該算是肥沃的農莊，越離開印威內斯，越靠蘇格蘭的海岸，蘇格蘭高地特有的荒涼景色就在車窗外展現出來。

在英國我們常看到大片草原，對於我們這種從城市來的人，這種草原已經夠賞心悅目了，可是這種草原一看就知道是有人照顧的，我就看過割草的自動化機器。真正的英國荒原，常常在較高的山嶺上，大都非常貧瘠，無法大規模地種植牧草，也不可能開發成森林，因此整個荒原上都覆蓋了野草和野花，使我百思不解的是這些野草並不亂長，它們貼著地長，簡直像我們在台灣故意種的朝鮮草，現在荒原上盛開一種叫做石楠的野花，淡紫色的，整個蘇格蘭的荒原上，現在幾

◇ breathtakingly（adv.）令人屏氣凝神地；氣都不敢喘地

◇ landscape（n.）（山川地貌的）景色；景緻

◇ unique [juˈnik]（adj.）別具特色的；自成一格的

◇ desolate（adj.）荒涼的；淒清苦冷的

the bottom often appeared, reflecting the mountains by the lakeside. As the setting sun sank westward, it was breathtakingly beautiful.

Our train left Inverness in a heavy fog, through which we could indistinctly see bluish-green pastures. Despite the fog, there were already people on horseback riding slowly over the plains. The train headed north at first, just as the red sun rose over the fog in the east. Plains, groves of trees, cows and sheep eating grass— this sort of landscape continued for an hour.

Inverness is quite a nice city. The plains around it aren't really moorland, but more like fertile farmland. The farther away from Inverness we got, the nearer we were to the coast. The unique, desolate scenery of the Scottish highlands began to appear outside the train windows.

In Britain we often saw vast, grassy plains that to us city-dwellers were refreshing enough, but it was obvious that those plains were tended by human hands— I even saw a lawnmower. The real British moorland is usually found on relatively high mountains. The land there tends to be quite infertile, so it can neither be extensively planted with pasture grass nor developed into forest; thus, the whole moorland is covered with wild grass and wildflowers. What I really couldn't understand is why this wild grass didn't grow irregularly— it was nice and short, just like the Zoysia grass we plant intentionally in

◇ obvious（adj.）明白的；顯然的

◇ extensively（adv.）廣泛地；大規模地

◇ infertile（adj.）貧瘠的；不肥沃的

◇ intentionally（adv.）有意地；特意地

平全被這種盛開的野花所覆蓋著，沒有野花的地方，就被像絲絨般的綠草所覆蓋。

11-15　　蘇格蘭的荒原的另一特色是多湖，不知何故，這些湖都是細長型的，兩旁常有高山、湖水永遠清澈見底。歐洲大陸也有有名的湖，可是這些湖都被商業化了，摩登的旅館會在湖邊出現，這種湖就不美了。蘇格蘭的湖邊不僅看不到什麼大旅館，連普通住家都不多，可是總會有一個古堡的廢墟坐落在湖邊，黃昏的夕陽之下這些古堡替蘇格蘭的湖平添了淒涼的美，難怪蘇格蘭的湖常常引起人們浪漫的遐思，〈羅莽湖畔〉這首悅耳的蘇格蘭民謠因此風行了整個世界。

　　到蒼穹島的火車之旅在最後一段，就完全沿著一個湖緩緩滑行，有一個車站造在湖邊，車停了，火車上僅有的幾個旅客都下來散散步，連列車長也下來了，一直等到他一催再催，我們才上車，在這裡火車通了人性，會等這些想散步的旅客。

◇ teeming（adj.）繁盛的；興茂的
◇ distinguishing（adj.）有所分野的；有特色的
◇ loch（n.）蘇格蘭地區稱 lake 為 loch
◇ commercialize（v.）商業化
◇ inspire（v.）啟發（某種）靈感；興起（某種）心念
◇ stroll（n.）漫步；閒逛

Taiwan. At that time, the moorland was teeming with a blooming light purple wildflower called heather; its blossoms practically blanketed the entire Scottish plain. The places where there were no wildflowers were covered with velvety grass.

Another distinguishing feature of the Scottish moorland is the large number of lochs. For some reason these lochs are all long and narrow, often with high mountains on both sides, and the water is always so clear you can see the bottom. There are famous lakes on the European mainland as well, but these lakes have all been commercialized: modern hotels appear on the lakeshore. That kind of lake is not beautiful. Not only do you not see motels by Scottish lochs, but even ordinary houses are fairly few there. There is always the ruin of some ancient castle situated by the lakeshore, however, and in the evening sunlight these castles add a desolate beauty to the lochs. No wonder lochs in Scotland have often inspired romantic fantasies: hence the beautiful Scottish folk song "Loch Lomond" that became world famous.

11-15
CD1-10

For the last part of the rail journey to Skye, we crept along slowly beside a loch. There was a station by the lakeshore; the train stopped there, and the few travelers on it all came out for a stroll. Even the conductor got out and waited for a while until, at his repeated urgings, we finally got back on the train. The trains there were very accommodating; they would wait for those of us travelers who wanted to take a stroll.

◇ urging(s)(n.)催趕；敦促
◇ accommodating(adj.)牽就的；配合的；通融的；給人方便的

　　下了火車，有渡輪在等，免費的，大約有十輛汽車在渡輪上，步行的旅客只有我們二人。到了蒼穹島，一輛又老又舊的紅色公共汽車在等我們，我買了來回票，票子其實是一張收據，我這個人向來糊裡糊塗，一拿了就丟，怎麼樣也找不到，其實我後來在褲子後面的口袋裡找到了，賣票給我的司機叫我不要著急，他到了站以後，拿一張紙，寫上票價，簽了名，填上日期，這張簽了名的紙，後來果然有用。可以作為回程票用。

　　蒼穹島的確是一個荒島，這裡只有一兩間好的旅館，這些旅館的造型像有錢人的家，島上有四百英里的道路，絕大多數的道路兩旁，都曠無人野，偶爾可以看到一兩座白色的鄉村小屋，小屋外面永遠有個修整得極為美麗的花園，英國人喜歡種花，島上有一個很大的花圃，供應各種的花，每一個鄉村小屋花園裡之所以有這麼多盛開的花，其實不是他們自己種的，而是到花圃去買現成的。

　　蒼穹島的中央是山，而且是荒山，英國政府在這裡造了一些林，虧得沒有大規模地造林，否則蒼穹島就沒有那種蒼涼之美，也就因為這些山上沒有樹，只有青草和野花，再加上很多山都只是丘陵而已，蒼

◇ receipt(n.)收據
◇ valid(adj.)有(法律)效力的

◇ model(after)(v.)仿效；師法；以……為本

After we alighted from the train, there was a free ferry waiting, on which there were about ten automobiles; the two of us were the only ones traveling on foot. Upon our arrival in Skye, an old, worn-out red bus was waiting for us. I bought a round trip ticket that was in fact a receipt. Being the clueless person I am, I lost it as soon as I got it and couldn't find it again no matter how hard I tried. (Actually, I later found it in the back pocket of my pants.) The driver who sold me the ticket told me to relax. After he got to the station, he took a piece of paper, wrote down the ticket price, signed his name and filled in the date. Sure enough, that signed piece of paper turned out to be valid: it served as my return ticket.

Skye really was a wild island; there were only one or two good motels there, modeled after rich people's houses. There were four hundred miles of road on the island, most of which were lined by unpopulated moorland on both sides. Occasionally you could see a white cottage or two, outside of which there would always be an exquisitely tended garden. The British enjoy planting flowers, and there was a huge flower nursery on the island that supplied all kinds of them. The cottage gardens were filled with so many blossoms not because the inhabitants had planted them themselves, but because they had bought them pre-grown from the nursery.

In the center of Skye were mountains— wild mountains. The British government once planted some groves of trees there, but fortunately not on a large scale, or else Skye would have lost its

◇ unpopulated（adj.）無人居住的；沒有人煙的
◇ exquisitely（adv.）（小巧）精緻地；精美細膩地

穹島最適合我們這種想爬山，又不能登高山的人，我們可以隨時隨地看到一座山，就上去走走。

16-20　我來以前，知道蒼穹島上有一個叫做「史都老人」的石柱，遠遠看這根石柱像美國首都華盛頓紀念碑，可是卻直立在一座高山之上，這次我沒有時間爬上去，看來也不是那麼難爬，下次我一定要去試試看。

　　幾年前，我看過一部史恩‧康納來演的電影，這個電影的外景全在蘇格蘭高地拍的，我這一次總算也在蒼穹島上登上了一個山頂，在我面前，蒼穹島的荒原一覽無遺，蘇格蘭人自稱蘇格蘭是蒼鷹仍然在飛的地方，可是我幾乎可以想像自己是一隻蒼鷹，因為我可以看得如此之遠，極目所望，看不到一個人，一輛汽車，甚至一幢房子，除了風聲以外，我也聽不到任何其他的聲音，大地一片靜寂。在我的心靈深處卻響起了英國民謠〈但尼少年〉，尤其其中「當山谷靜靜地覆上了層白雪」那句話最能描寫我當時的心情。

◇ the Washington Monument 華盛頓紀念碑（是美國首都華盛頓最高的建築物，為一座方尖塔，內有美國國父華盛頓塑像）
◇ definitely（adv.）確定地；當然地
◇ film（v.）（電影）拍攝；入鏡

unique form of desolate beauty. Precisely because these mountains had no trees— only green grass and wildflowers— and many of them were only hills, Skye was perfect for those of us who wanted to go hiking but couldn't hike up high mountains. Whenever and wherever we saw a mountain, we could go up and walk around on it.

Before I came, I knew that Skye had a stone pillar called the Old Man of Storr. From far away, the pillar looked like the Washington Monument of America's capital city, but it was standing on a high mountain. This time I didn't have time to climb up, although it looked like it wouldn't be that tough to climb. Next time I'm definitely going to try.

16-20

A few years ago, I watched a movie starring Sean Connery in which the outdoor scenes were all filmed in the Scottish highlands. Now I could finally say that I too had climbed to the top of a mountain of Skye. Before my eyes, the moorland of the isle unfolded in its entirety. Scots claim that Scotland is a place where eagles still fly. I could almost imagine myself as an eagle then, for I could see so incredibly far. Everywhere my eyes could reach, I saw not a single person, a single car, or even a single house. Besides the wind, I could hear no other sound; the world was a sweeping expanse of tranquility. Deep in my heart, though, there sounded the English folk song "Danny Boy," especially the part about "when the valley's hushed and white with snow." That line is the best description of my feelings at that time.

◇ unfold (v.) 開展；延伸開來（原著英譯 Before me eyes, the wildness of the isle unfolded in its entirety. 此句相當於中文「小島荒原景色在我面前一覽無遺」。）

◇ sweeping (adj.) 廣闊的；浩瀚的；連綿的

蒼穹島的回程公車上，只有我一個客人，我一面對著窗外令我無限懷念的荒涼景色說再見，一面想些話題和司機聊天。司機的駕駛座旁邊放了一盒巧克力糖，他看我好心和他聊天，請我吃了兩顆巧克力糖。

第二天，我告別了蘇格蘭，去拜訪勃朗特姐妹的故居，勃朗特姐妹至少有兩位是我們所熟知的，夏洛蒂·勃朗特是《簡愛》的作者，愛米兒·勃朗特是《咆哮山莊》的作者，他們的故居在英格蘭北部叫做哈華斯小鎮附近的荒原，是很多旅客喜歡去散步的地方。

去哈華斯，我要換幾次火車，最後一次火車的旅程，只有二十分鐘，卻是蒸汽火車，這是整個英國碩果僅存的幾條蒸汽火車鐵路，車子奇舊無比，服務員、連司機在內，都是義工。他們向政府力爭要維持住這些蒸汽火車，雖然乘客已經不多，可是由於由義工來服務，居然也還能夠撐了下去。

21-25　　使我感歎的是鐵路沿線的小火車站，雖然小到了極點，可是極為雅致，火車站上仍然種滿了花，車站的燈飾也維持住當年的古典型式。

◇ well-intentioned（adj.）好心的；善意的　　◇ residence（n.）居所；住處

On the return bus trip, I was the only passenger. As I said a very reluctant goodbye to the desolate scenery, I thought of some things to chat about with the driver. There was a box of chocolates beside the driver's seat; out of gratitude for my well-intentioned effort to make conversation, he gave me a couple of the chocolates.

On the second day, I bade farewell to Scotland and went to visit the former residence of the Brontë sisters, at least two of whom we're familiar with: Charlotte Brontë is the author of *Jane Eyre*, and Emily Brontë is the author of *Wuthering Heights*. Their old house is in the moorland around the northern English town of Haworth; it's a place where many travelers like to go walking.

CD1-11

To get to Haworth, I had to change trains several times. The last train ride only lasted twenty minutes, but it was on a steam train. This was one of the few remaining steam railroads in Britain. The cars were incredibly old, and the workers, including the engineer, were all volunteers who had struggled with the government to preserve these steam trains. Even though passengers were few, because the trains were staffed by volunteers, they still managed to stay in business.

What really impressed me were the little train stations along the line: although they were about as small as could be, they were extremely elegant, still adorned with the teeming flowerbeds and antique lighting of their heyday.

21-25

◇ remaining (adj.) 剩餘的；留存的　　◇ antique [æn'tik] (adj.) 古色古香的；懷古的

　　我走出了哈華斯車站，大約是晚上七點左右，發現街上一個人也沒有，好不容易找到幾個「臥床和早餐」的牌子，卻找不到主人。在英國旅行，大多數人喜歡住人家家裡，這些經過政府發給執照的家庭，在門口掛上「臥床和早餐」的牌子，一個旅客只收十五英鎊左右(大約等於台幣六百六十元)，除了臥室以外，還可以享受一頓熱騰騰的英國式早餐。我在失望之餘，忽然看到一個「小屋出租」的牌子，也看到有人在裡面吃晚飯，就硬了頭皮去敲門了。

　　應門的是一對五十多歲的夫婦，他們說他們的確有一幢小屋出租，可是都是租給一家人的，而且一租就租一週。所以對於我這個人只要住一個晚上，不免有點面有難色。可是經過我苦苦哀求以後，男主人說「我們總不能讓這個可憐的年輕人(我已五十三歲)流浪街頭」，於是我總算找到了一間屋子過夜。

　　哈華斯小鎮是個典型英國美麗的小鎮，全鎮只有一條石鋪的小街，兩旁的建築全是石造的古屋，連街燈也像古色古香的煤氣燈，雖然很美，可是入夜以後空盪盪的街上只剩下我一個人，小鎮旁荒原上的霧

◇ discouraged (adj.) 灰心的；沮喪的　　　　◇ hesitant (adj.) 遲疑的；猶豫不決的

When I walked out of the Haworth station at about seven in the evening, I discovered there was not a single person in the streets. After a good bit of searching, I found a few bed and breakfast signs, but I couldn't find the hosts. (Most people like to stay in other people's houses while traveling in Britain. These families, licensed by the government, hang "bed and breakfast" signs in their doorways, and for just fifteen pounds [about NT$660], a traveler can enjoy a piping hot English breakfast in addition to a place to sleep.) Just as I was getting really discouraged, I saw a sign that said "small house for rent" at a place where there were people having dinner inside. I forced myself to go knock on their door.

A couple in their fifties answered the door. They said they did in fact have a small house for rent, but it was meant for an entire family, and they rented it out for a week at a time. Faced with someone like me who only wanted to stay for a night, it was hard to blame them for being a bit hesitant. After I begged them to let me stay, however, the man said, "Well, we can't leave this poor lad (I was already fifty-three) to wander through the streets." And that was how I finally found myself a place to spend the night.

Haworth was a beautiful small town in the classic English style. There was only one stone-paved street in the whole town, and the masonry buildings along both sides were all very old. Even the streetlights seemed for all the world like real coal lamps from former times. Although it was beautiful, being the only person in the deserted streets after nightfall as the fog blew in from the surrounding

◇ deserted (adj.) 空無一人的；沒有人跡的

卻一陣陣地吹來，不禁使我想起了描寫英國謀殺案的電影(我才看過「開膛手傑克」那部影片)。

我租的小屋其實不小，樓下是起居室和飯廳，樓上有四間臥室，我糊裡糊塗地一個人住進了這幢屋子，卻又想起了《咆哮山莊》裡荒野裡女主角鬼魂的呼叫聲，不禁害怕起來，入睡以前，我做了一件丟臉的事，我打開了走廊的燈，這樣總比整個屋子漆黑一片好。

26-30　哈華斯小鎮是當年勃朗特姐妹居住的地方，他們的父親是一位牧師，全家住的那幢石造的房子依然存在，已成為博物館。小鎮附近全是田野和荒原，因為地勢很高，當地風很大，入冬以後更是蕭瑟得緊，可是英國人偏偏喜歡到野外去散步，勃朗特姐妹們生前常常到附近的荒原去散步，我曾看過她們的傳記，發現她們全部英年早逝，好像都是死於肺炎(或肺病)，顯然在寒冷的天氣裡到荒原去散步，雖然可以得到文學上的靈感，可是對健康一定不太好，難怪我們的作家們很少去荒原散步了。

傳說愛米兒‧勃朗特生前常沿著一條荒涼的步道去探訪一座農莊，這座農莊築在高地，附近盡是荒野，由於視野遼闊，愛米兒一定喜歡

◇ pitch black(dark)黑漆漆的；伸手不見五指的　　◇ curate [ˈkjurɪt](n.)堂區牧師

moorland, I couldn't help thinking of movies about English murder cases (I had just recently watched the movie *Jack the Ripper*).

The small house I had rented was actually not small at all. The lower floor had a sitting room and dining room, and the upper floor had four bedrooms. Like a fool, I had moved into this house all alone. I then thought of the cries of the heroine's ghost in *Wuthering Heights* and became frightened in spite of myself. Before going to sleep, I did a shameful thing: I turned on the hall light. At least that felt better than the whole house being pitch black.

Haworth was where the Brontë sisters lived back in their day. Their father was a curate, and the stone house in which the family used to live is still standing today. It has become a museum. The town is surrounded by farm fields and moorland. Because the terrain there is high, the wind blows hard, so it's quite chilly, especially in the winter. Despite their poor weather, however, the British still enjoy going for walks outdoors. The Brontë sisters would often go walking on the neighboring moor. I once read a biography of them and discovered that all three died young, of pneumonia (or lung disease). Evidently, although strolling through the moorland in cold weather can bring literary inspiration, it's definitely not good for the health. No wonder our authors seldom go for strolls in the wilderness.

26-30

Legend has it that Emily Brontë used to walk along a desolate trail to visit a large farm. This farm was built on high ground and

◇ standing (adj.) (建築物等) 仍然存在的　　◇ inspiration (n.) 靈感；靈思
◇ evidently (adv.) 明白地；顯然地

來此尋求靈感，她的《咆哮山莊》就是根據這座荒原上的農莊而寫出來的。

我到哈華斯，主要的目的就是去探訪那座農莊，農莊距離小鎮有五公里，必須步行才能到達，我一早到當地的旅客資料中心去拿了一張地圖，按著地圖去找，好在這條有名的勃朗特步道沿路有指標，除了英文以外，還有中文，不會迷路，可是只有我一個人，未免有些寂寞。好不容易看到了一對老夫婦從反方向散步回來，趕快問他們咆哮山莊究竟在哪裡，老人指給我看，我不禁倒抽一口冷氣，因為那座孤伶伶的農莊看起來遙遠得不得了，可望而不可及，老人看我有點心虛，立刻鼓勵我，「年輕人，再走一小時就到了」，在洋老人面前豈可退縮，我只好硬著頭皮向前走去。

到了那座叫做勃朗特小橋的地方，我總算看到了一位白衣女郎，而且是東方人，在我前面一段路，這下我精神為之一振，加緊腳步趕去，沒有料到前面有一段筆直的山路要爬，這一段路爬下來，我已經

◇ tourist information center 旅遊資訊中心；遊客服務處

◇ opposite(adj.)**反方向的；相對的**

surrounded by moorland. Because the view was so magnificent, Emily must have loved going there in search of inspiration. She used this farm above the moorland as the basis for her *Wuthering Heights*.

CD1-12

The main reason I had gone to Haworth was to visit that farm, which was situated five Kilometers out of town and could only be reached on foot. In the morning, I went to the local tourist information center to get a map, which I followed toward the farm. Fortunately, the famous Brontë trail had signs all along it that were written in Chinese as well as English, so it was impossible to get lost. Being all alone, however, I couldn't help feeling a bit lonely. After quite a bit of looking, I saw an elderly couple walking in the opposite direction. Hurriedly I asked them where exactly Wuthering Heights was. When the old man pointed it out for me, I couldn't help gasping with discouragement, for that solitary manor house looked so remote, so easy to look at yet so hard to reach. The old man saw that I looked somewhat crestfallen, so he immediately encouraged me: "Just walk another hour, lad, and you'll be there." How could I turn back in front of elderly foreigners? I had no choice but to grit my teeth and press forward.

When I got to the place called Brontë Bridge, I finally saw a young woman in white, an Easterner at that, on the trail ahead of me. At that moment my spirits rose, and I quickened my step and hurried onward. I had not expected, however, to find a straight road up the mountain ahead of me to climb. After I got through that part, I was half-dead

◇ solitary (adj.) 遺世獨立的；自己一人的　　◇ crestfallen (adj.) 垂頭喪氣的

氣喘如牛，半條命送掉，最糟糕的是那位白衣女郎和我的距離越來越遠。

　　這條步道一開始時還在牧場中穿過，路旁也可以看到疏疏落落的家屋，大約半小時以後，就完全是真正的荒原了，到了咆哮山莊，才發現這座農莊在山頂，雖然整個山谷都可以看得一清二楚，可是山谷裡沒有一幢房子，沒有一點人工的痕跡，看不完的紫色石楠花在微風中搖擺，我不懂為什麼會有人在這裡造座農莊，唯一的理由恐怕就是要享受四週原野的靜寂，可是在秋冬這裡會被大雪覆蓋，再加上大風，住在咆哮山莊的主人必定喜歡與世隔絕。在我走完這一段路程的時候，我內心裡暗暗佩服愛米兒‧勃朗特，她這麼一位弱女子，居然常常花上幾小時在荒原中散步，她們三姐妹之所以能成為著名的作家，不知與她們的荒野散步有無關係。

31-33　　在咆哮山莊，我找到了那位白衣女郎，是位日本人。虧得她幫我照了一張相，照相的時候，一頭黑臉羊過來和我親熱(有相片為證)，使我感到溫馨無比。回程和這位年輕的女孩子同行，她健步如飛，我

◇ gap(n.)溝(註：本指斷裂處所形成的溝，譬如 generation gap 為「代溝」而 information gap 則指的是「知識落差」或「資訊斷層」。在英譯裡...and the worst thing was that the gap between me and the woman in white was widening. 此處 gap 指的是一前一後兩位旅者間的距離)

and panting like a dog, and the worst thing was that the gap between me and the woman in white was widening.

At first, the trail went through pasture, and you could see a few houses here and there by the side of the road; half an hour later, however, it was all moorland. After I got to the manor of Wuthering Heights, I discovered that the farm was on a mountaintop. Even though you could see the whole valley as clearly as could be, there wasn't a single house in the valley, and no sign of anything manmade. The endless purple heather swayed in the wind. I couldn't understand why anyone would want to build a farm here— I'm afraid the only reason must have been to enjoy the tranquility of the plains all around. But still, in the autumn and winter this place would be covered in deep snow and buffeted by strong winds. The master of Wuthering Heights must have enjoyed being cut off from the world. After I finished my hike, I inwardly admired Emily Brontë— though she was only a frail girl, she regularly spent hours walking in the moorland. I wonder if the three sisters' literary success had anything to do with their habit of strolling through the moorland?

At Wuthering Heights, I found that woman in white. She was Japanese, and she was kind enough to take a picture for me. When she was about to take it, a black-faced sheep came over and nuzzled up to me (I have the picture to prove it), which made me feel all warm

31-33

◇ sway (v.) (左右或前後) 搖擺
◇ tranquility [træŋ`kwɪlətɪ] (n.) 寧靜
◇ buffet [`bʌfɪt] (v.) (指風、雨、雪) 迎面猛烈吹襲

◇ nuzzle (v.) (指動物或人撒嬌或親膩地用鼻子) 挨近或磨蹭

兩度叫停，丟盡了臉，不過我比她大了三十歲，能在三小時走完十公里，已經算是不錯了。

告別了荒原，我回到了倫敦，脫下旅行時穿的流浪漢衣服，打上領帶，穿上西裝，恢復我名教授的身分，有模有樣地在旅館餐廳裡和其他幾位名教授吃晚飯。侍者禮貌之至，可是一點表情也沒有；菜肴精緻之至，可是一點味道也沒有，就在這個時刻，餐廳忽然播放了維瓦弟的〈四季〉，我的心又立刻飛回了微風輕拂的無邊荒原，我輕輕地告訴它們，只要你們一直是荒原，只要蒼鷹仍在盤旋，我一定會回來的。

親愛的讀者，如果你喜歡享受荒原之美，千萬不要告訴你庸俗的朋友，如果蒼穹島上有了希爾頓酒店和麥當勞，一切都完了。

◇ identity（n.）身分
◇ epitome [ɪˋpɪtəmɪ]（n.）象徵；表徵；具體而微所呈現出來的人或物（註：以原譯 the waiters were the epitome of courtesy 而言，意思為「侍者把殷勤有禮具體而微地呈現出來」，也就是「侍者非常之謙恭有禮」的意思）

inside. On the way back I walked with this young woman. She flew along with lively steps, while I embarrassed myself by asking her to stop twice. I was thirty years older than she, though— walking ten kilometers in three hours was really not bad for me.

I said farewell to the moorland and headed back to London, where I took off the wanderer's clothes I had worn while traveling, tied my tie, put on my suit and reassumed my identity as a famous professor. Just like a famous professor should, I had dinner with other famous professors at the restaurant in my hotel. The waiters were the epitome of courtesy, but their faces were totally expressionless; the food was the height of sophistication, but it was utterly tasteless. At that moment, Vivaldi's *Four Seasons* began playing in the restaurant, and my heart immediately flew back to the boundless moorland caressed by the gentle breeze. I whispered to it that as long as it never ceased being moorland— as long as eagles still circled there— I would surely return.

Dear reader, if you enjoy admiring the beauty of the moorland, whatever you do, never tell your vulgar friends about it. If Hilton and McDonald's ever come to the Isle of Skye, we're done for.

◇ sophistication(n.)精緻；(手工或火候)精巧(註：以原譯 the food was the height of sophistication 而言，意思為「食物呈現出來高層次的精美程度」，也就是「食物精美之至」的意思」)
◇ boundless(adj.)無涯無際的
◇ circle(v.)盤旋；兜圈子

(1) go blind（deaf, pale, numb, limp, ...）變瞎（聾、蒼白、麻痺、跛行）（3段）

After the main male character goes blind, he still calls out the heroine's name to the moorland.

男主角眼睛瞎了以後，仍然對著荒原呼叫女主角的名字。

解析

人「變」瞎了、聾了；臉色「變」白了；身體「變」強壯了、虛弱了、麻痺了、癱軟了；天色「變」昏暗了、明亮了；天氣「變」好了、壞了；牛奶「變」酸了；食品「變」質了。諸如以上的這些「變」字，都可以用 go 這個字來表達。別忘了，掛在英美人士口邊的一句話是：Things went terribly wrong. 讀者應該可以從這個句子裡頭 went 的用法而聯想到以上種種的「變」法吧！就用這樣子的思考來做以下兩個練習。

小試身手

1. 電池（變得）沒電了。

　_____

2. 麵包（變得）（酸腐）壞掉了。

　_____

---

(2) one... the other... 一個⋯⋯（而）另一個⋯⋯（5段）

One was the Isle of Skye, off the western coast of Scotland; the other was the Haworth moorland, ...

一個是蘇格蘭西海岸的蒼穹島，一個是哈華斯荒原。

解析

學習者要特別注意，使用這個句型的前提為總數是兩個的情況。你有兩個禮物，一個要送爸爸，另一個要送媽媽，以英文表示就要寫成：I have bought two gifts. One is intended for Father and the other（is intended）for Mother.

小試身手

3. 兩個交戰國家宗教信仰各自不同。一個為基督教國家，一個為回教國家。

_____

---

(3) It is a pity that... 很令人惋惜……；很令人遺憾……（6段）

He said that it was a pity it wasn't raining that night...
他說可惜今晚不下雨。

解析

這個句型是指一件「令人感到遺憾的事」或是「令人覺得可惜的事」，整個句型基本上是一個虛主詞 it 和真主詞 that 子句兩者間的關係。比如現在我們想表達「很令人遺憾他錢賺得不夠他花」，那就得把「他錢賺得不夠他花」寫成一個 that 子句（即：that he spends money faster than he makes it），然後把它放在 It is a pity 的後面，就形成 It is a pity that he spends money faster than he makes it.

小試身手

4. 那座古堡毀於地震，很令人惋惜。

_____

（4）... so... that... ⋯⋯到（足以）⋯⋯（7段）

Along the way, lakes so clear (that) you could see the bottom often appeared, reflecting the mountains by the lakeside.

途中常有清澈見底的湖出現，將這些山倒映在湖邊。

解析

這是一個和文法觀念有關的句型，... so... that... 為從屬連接詞，在比較口語的場合可以考慮把 that 省略，所引導的子句稱之為「結果副詞子句」，用以表示某種特性達到某種程度（so...），以致造成某種結果（that...）。比方說某人身體很虛，虛到連說話的力氣都沒有，這樣的情況如何表示呢？我們就來演練一下吧。

小試身手

5. 那個病人身體虛弱到連說話的力氣都沒有。

_____

（5）介詞＋關係代名詞 ... through which...（8段）

Our train left Inverness in a heavy fog, through which we could indistinctly see bluish-green pastures.

我們的火車，在大霧中離開了印威內斯城，依依稀稀地可以看到翠綠的牧場。

解析

大概一般人都可看得出來，關係代名詞 which 指的就是前面的 heavy fog，問題在於為什麼關係代名詞前面還要加上一個介詞 through 呢？這時你可就要往後面看了，注意到後半句的動詞（see）嗎？它和 through 兩者合起來，形成「看穿」、「看透」，你說，沒有 through 行嗎？

6. 我匆匆走過校門，圍在校門附近有許多人群聚在哪裡。

_____

(6) The ADJer..., the ADJer... 越（是）……越（是）……（9段）

The farther away from Inverness we got, the nearer we were to the coast.
越離開印威內斯，越靠蘇格蘭的海岸。

解析

這是個很費解的結構，前後定冠詞 (the) 的用法很特殊，也不是它平常的意思，不是英語母語人士恐怕要花些時間適應，慶幸的是這個結構並不囉嗦，而且中文也有類似的說法，如「梅花越冷越開花」、「某人越大規矩越差」。別忘了兩個 the 的後面要使用比較級。

7. 我看他越久，我越害怕。

_____

(7) 倒裝句型：Not only do（does）+ S. + Vrt... but... 不只……而且……（11段）

Not only do you not see motels by Scottish lakes, but even ordinary houses are fairly few there.
蘇格蘭的湖邊不僅看不到什麼大旅館，連普通住家都不多。

解析

我相信所有的人即使英文很破，也知道 not only... but also... 這個句型。可是認識歸認識，這個句型也有它特殊之處，當 not only 被放到句首時，因為它本身具否定含意，會影響到後面主詞和動詞的順序，即需要用倒裝結構，以原譯文而言就表現在 (...do you not see...)。

小試身手

8. 他不只會創作詩而且菜煮得很好。

_____

(8) 分詞構句：Ving..., S. + V. +... ⋯⋯到（足以）⋯⋯（13段）

Being the clueless person I am, I lost it as soon as I got it and couldn't find it again no matter how hard I tried.

我這個人向來糊裡糊塗，一拿了就丟，怎麼樣也找不到。

解析

這是純屬文法觀念的句型，從文法的角度看，這原本是一個從屬子句 (As I am a clueless person) 和主要子句 (I lost it as soon as I got it and couldn't find it again no matter how hard I tried) 合成的句子，如果我們要減少一個子句，就可以考慮把從屬連接詞和主詞省略，然後把動詞化為分詞。以原譯文而論，連接詞 (As) 和主詞 (I) 省略後，再把原來的動詞 (am) 變成分詞 (Being)，其他部分則保持不變，最後的結果 (Being the clueless person I am) 就是所謂的分詞構句。

藉以下練習來領略箇中道理；建議你寫兩個句子，第一句把放在括弧裡的「雖然」和「她」寫進去；第二句則把它們省略。

小試身手

9. （雖然）（她）知道他不會來了，她還是繼續等了兩個鐘頭。

(1) _____

(2) _____

（9） Even though... 儘管……；縱然……（20段）

Even though passengers were few, because the trains were staffed by volunteers, they surprisingly still managed to stay in business.

雖然乘客已經不多，可是由於由義工來服務，居然也還能夠撐了下去。

解析

在意思上為「儘管」、「縱然」，在文法上的作用它是從屬連接詞，後面跟著主詞和動詞等以形成從屬子句，原譯文裡的 Even though passengers were few 就是從屬子句，這種由 (even though / though / although) 之類的字帶頭形成的從屬子句，文法上給它一個很特殊的稱呼，叫作「讓步副詞子句」。

小試身手

10. 雖然她其貌不揚，可是她很受同校男孩子歡迎。

_____

（10） as... as can（could）be... ……到不能再……（21段）

Although they were about as small as could be, they were extremely elegant...

雖然小到了極點，可是極為雅致……

解析

這是一個很值得學的句型，即使是在使用中文的時候，我們不也常語帶誇張地說「大到不能再大了」、「美到不能到美了」這類的話。如果你想要用英文表示，別忘了，就是這個句型。

小試身手

11. 這些動畫人物真是可愛到不能再可愛了(可愛到不行)。

＿＿＿＿＿＿＿＿＿＿＿＿＿＿＿＿＿＿＿＿＿＿＿＿＿

(11) piping hot 燒燙燙；熱騰騰(22段)

... and for just fifteen pounds(about NT$660), travelers can enjoy a piping hot English breakfast in addition to a place to sleep.

……一個旅客只收十五英鎊左右(大約等於台幣六百六十元)，除了臥室以外，還可以享受一頓熱騰騰的英國式早餐。

解析

人類語言的共通性有時真讓我們驚訝，中文說「冷冰冰」、「軟綿綿」、「熱騰騰」、「慢吞吞」，這些疊字的效果，讓人更加會心地瞭解「冷」、「軟」、「熱」、「慢」。英文也不遑多讓，除了原譯文以表示 piping hot「熱騰騰」，我們也可以用 scorching hot 或 burning hot 表示「熱烘烘」，通常用來指酷熱難當的天氣，用 freezing cold 表示「冷冰冰」，用 bone-piercing cold 表示「寒徹骨」。

小試身手

12. 我們進去吧！外面冷冰冰的。

＿＿＿＿＿＿＿＿＿＿＿＿＿＿＿＿＿＿＿＿＿＿＿＿＿

（12）... blame somebody for... 責怪（某人）……（23段）

Faced with someone like me who only wanted to stay for a night, it was hard to blame them for being a bit hesitant.

對於我這個人只要住一個晚上，不免有點面有難色。

解析

這個句型恰好相當於中文「怪罪某人某事」，blame 是「譴責怪罪」的意思，介詞 for 則表示遭到譴責怪罪的原因。譯者在這裡用 it was hard to blame them for being a bit hesitant（很難怪罪他們有點猶豫）來處理原著裡的「不免有點面有難色」。

小試身手

13. 他常常莫名其妙怪罪別人。

_____

（13）in spite of oneself 身不由己；不由自主（25段）

but then I thought of the cries of the heroine's ghost in *Wuthering Heights* and became frightened in spite of myself.

卻又想起了《咆哮山莊》裡荒野裡女主角鬼魂的呼叫聲，不禁害怕起來。

解析

讀者們先要革除一個對這個片語先入為主的觀念，以為 in spite of 就一定作「儘管」、「雖然」解釋，相反的，in spite of oneself 在這裡的意思是「控制不了自己」的意思。

小試身手

14. 我百般克制但還是害怕的發抖。

_____

(14) Legend has it that... 民間傳說⋯⋯；鄉野奇譚⋯⋯(27段)

Legend has it that Emily Brontë used to walk along a desolate trail to visit a large farm.

傳說愛米兒‧勃朗特生前常沿著一條荒涼的步道去探訪一座農莊。

解析

歷經長久時間的流傳說法，難以考證其真偽者，英文用 Legend has it that... 若是市井八卦口耳相傳，搞得沸沸揚揚，同時也一樣真偽難辨，英文用 Rumor has it that... 來表達，意思為「謠言說⋯⋯」、「謠傳⋯⋯」。

小試身手

15. 八卦消息說那位女歌手三年前就結婚了。

_____

(15) be situated... 位於⋯⋯；坐落在⋯⋯(28段)

The main reason I had gone to Haworth was to visit that farm, which was situated five miles out of town and could only be reached on foot.

我到哈華斯，主要的目的就是去探訪那座農莊，農莊距離小鎮有五公里，必須步行才能到達。

解析

要表示某個建築物的地理位置在某地方，可以使用這個句型，特別注意用的是 be situated 這樣的形式，後面則視情況使用如 in 或 on 或 at 之類的介詞。

小試身手

16. 第一家星巴克就在蔬菜市場對面。

_____

---

(16) have no choice but to V... 別無選擇只能……；不得不……
（28段）

How could I turn back in front of elderly foreigners? I had no choice but to grit my teeth and press forward.

在洋老人面前豈可退縮，我只好硬著頭皮向前走去。

解析

have no choice 當然很容易理解，就是「沒有選擇」的意思，比較費解的是跟在後面的 but，這個 but 當「除了……」，後面接著不定詞 (to V)，整個綜合起來的意思為「除了（做……）已沒有選擇」。

小試身手

17. 面臨鉅額虧損，那家公司不得不宣布破產。

_____

（17）**the epitome of courtesy** 極其有禮

　　　the height of sophistication 極其精緻（32段）

The waiters were the epitome of courtesy, but their faces were totally expressionless; the food was the height of sophistication, but it was tasteless.

侍者禮貌之至，可是一點表情也沒有；菜肴精緻之至，可是一點味道也沒有。

[解析]

這種句型讀者可要花點時間和心思去體會，中文裡有「……之至」或「……至極」的說法，比如「無恥之至」和「無禮至極」，英文也有，而表達起來就是 the epitome of... 或 the height of...

「無恥之至」：the epitome of shamelessness

「無禮至極」：the height of rudeness

[小試身手]

18. 在這座廟裡你可以欣賞到台灣民俗藝術的精髓。

_____

小試身手解答

1. The batteries went dead.

2. The bread went stale.

3. The two warring countries are different in their respective religious faiths. One is a Christian country and the other is a Muslim country.

4. It is a pity that the old castle was toppled in an earthquake.

5. The patient is so ill(weak) that he doesn't even have the strength to talk.

6. I hurried past the school gate, around which a large crowd had gathered.

7. The longer I looked at him, the more frightened I felt.

8. Not only can he compose poetry, but he is an exceptionally good cook.

9. (1) Although she knew that he would never appear, she continued to wait for two more hours.

   (2) Knowing that he would never appear, she continued to wait for two more hours.

10. Although she is plain, she is quite popular with the boys at school.

11. These animated characters are as cute as can be.

12. Let's go inside! It's freezing cold out here.

13. He often blames people for no reason.

14. I shook with fear in spite of myself.

15. Rumor has it that the female singer got married three years ago.

16. The first Starbucks was situated opposite the farmers' market.

17. Faced with massive losses, the company had no choice but to declare bankruptcy.

18. Here in this temple, you can admire the epitome of Taiwanese folk art.

Chef Wu's Feast

吳師傅的盛宴

1-5　　再過兩天就是農曆新年了，天氣好冷，如果打開報紙來看，我們會更覺得冷。

　　有一位新竹跑社會新聞的記者告訴我一個他的經驗，他說他的職業使他常常覺得非常沮喪，而他應付的辦法很簡單，他會去新竹縣鄉下的一個專門收容家遭變故孩子的兒童中心，這所兒童中心由一群善心的修女主持，她們的仁愛和贊助者的熱心常能使這位記者恢復對社會的信心。

　　我晚上正好有事去這所兒童中心，雖然只有兩個小時，我卻看到了好多善心人士來幫忙，一對老夫婦駕了一部小貨車來，車廂後門打開，一件一件的新夾克拿了出來。快過年了，這對老夫妻顯然認為過年時應該穿新衣服。

　　當晚我在家裡看了一部電影，「芭比的盛宴」，這部電影似乎在解釋一個簡單的道理，那就是人不能只靠崇高的理想過活，我們這些凡人有時也需要吃一些好的東西。芭比是一位名廚，她在電影裡所表演的那一場法國大餐不是給大人物吃的，而是為了一些鄉下人。

CD2-2
◇ freezing cold 冷冰冰的
◇ relate (v.) 敘述
◇ depressed (adj.) 沮喪的；失意的；鬱悶的

1-5
CD2-1

In another two days the Lunar New Year will be here, and the weather is freezing cold. If you take a look at the newspaper, you'll feel even colder.

A social news reporter in Hsinchu related an experience of his to me. He said his job often made him feel depressed, but he had a very simple way of coping: he would go to a rural part of Hsinchu County to visit a children's center dedicated to caring for kids from families hit by unexpected misfortunes. The center is run by a group of good-hearted nuns: seeing their kindness and the enthusiasm of the helpers there would restore the reporter's faith in society.

One evening I had business that took me to this children's center. Although I was there for a mere two hours, I saw a multitude of kindhearted people helping out. An elderly couple drove up in a little truck, opened the door at the back and took out new jackets one by one. New Year's was fast approaching, and clearly this couple thought that at New Year's one ought to have new clothes to wear.

At home later that night, I watched a movie called *Babette's Feast*. The movie seemed to be explaining a simple principle: man can't live on lofty ideals alone— at times, we ordinary people need to eat some good food. Babette was a famous chef, but the French banquet she made in the movie was not for VIPs; rather, it was for a few village folk.

◇ enthusiasm (n.) 熱忱；認真
◇ multitude (n.) 眾多；大群(的人或動物)
◇ principle (n.) 原則；原理
◇ banquet [ˈbæŋkwɪt] (n.) 大餐；盛宴

看完以後，我不禁想起那所兒童中心的孩子們，會不會有人做一頓好吃的年夜飯給他們吃呢？

6-10　　除夕，我在下午五點鐘還在辦公室假裝認真地工作，整個清華大學靜悄悄地。從我的電腦終端機上，忽然傳來一句話「老師，回家去吃年夜飯吧，我已關燈，馬上就要走了。」又一次提醒我年夜飯的事，中國人總要在這個除夕夜吃一頓特別的飯。

清華園到了現在，可謂萬籟俱寂。我忍不住開了車子在校園裡繞一圈，果真所有大樓裡的燈光全部都熄了，連宿舍也是靜悄悄地。路過第二招待所，卻發現裡面的餐廳熱鬧得很，走進去有些孩子在裡面看電視，再一看，我所說的那所兒童中心的徐修女帶著一大批孩子在看電視，她告訴我，第二招待所的吳師傅請她們全體小朋友吃年夜飯。

餐廳裡的餐桌上鋪了紅色的桌布，碗筷也比較講究，在廚房裡，吳大師傅和他的幾位助手，聚精會神地準備大餐。幾位我認識的僑生在

◇ delectable（adj.）可口的；好吃的
◇ pretend（v.）假裝
◇ screen（n.）（電視）螢光幕；（電影）銀幕

◇ dorm（s）（n.）宿舍（註：為 dormitory 的簡寫）

After I finished watching, I couldn't help thinking of the kids at that children's center. Would anyone fix a delectable New Year's Eve dinner for them?

On New Year's Eve, I was still in the office at five in the afternoon pretending to be working hard. All of Tsing Hua was quiet. Suddenly a message appeared on my computer screen: "Teacher, go home for New Year's dinner. I just turned off the lights and I'm about to leave." This once again reminded me of New Year's dinner— Chinese people always have a special meal on New Year's Eve.

6-10

By now, Tsing Hua was completely still. I couldn't resist taking a drive around the campus. Sure enough, all the lights in every building were out, and even the dorms were quiet. Passing by the No. 2 Reception Center, however, I discovered that the restaurant inside was as bustling as could be. I walked in and saw some kids watching TV. Upon closer inspection, I found that Nun Xu from the children's center I mentioned was inside chaperoning a group of children as they watched TV. She told me that Chef Wu, who worked at the reception center, was treating all the kids to New Year's dinner.

The tables in the restaurant were spread with red tablecloths, and the bowls and chopsticks were elegant, too. In the kitchen, Chef Wu and a few of his helpers were intently preparing a feast. A few overseas students I knew were lending a hand, one of whom was an

◇ bustling（adj.）熱鬧的；熙攘的；人聲鼎沸的
◇ inspection（n.）檢查；察看
◇ treat（v.）請客；招待
◇ intently（adv.）專注地；認真地；用心地

幫忙,有一位是學電機的,沒想到他除了設計積體電路以外,還會切豆腐乾。

我心裡感到無比的溫暖,出校門的時候,看到四位年輕的警衛在聊天,他們又是一批吃不到年夜飯的傢伙,我因此停下來和他們聊幾句。有一位警衛甚至和我輕鬆地開起玩笑來,我當然也回敬幾句,車子開走的時候,聽到一位警衛說「為什麼李老頭今天情緒特別好?」

當晚有人從台北打電話來,他說台北好冷,問我新竹如何。我說我不覺得冷,在一個互相關懷的社會裡,誰會覺得冷呢?

◇ design(v.)設計　　　　　　◇ integrated circuit(s)[ˋsɝkɪt] 積體電路

electronics student. I never knew that besides designing integrated circuits, he also knew how to slice dried tofu.

I felt deliciously warm inside. As I went out the school gate, I saw four young security guards chatting with each other. They were another group of guys who didn't get to eat a New Year's Eve dinner, so I stopped and joined in their conversation for a bit. One of them even casually joked around with me, so of course I did the same with him. As I drove away, I heard one of the guards say, "Why is Old Lee in such a good mood today?"

That night someone called from Taipei. He said it was freezing there, and he asked me how Hsinchu was. I said I didn't feel cold— in a society where people care for one another, why would anyone feel cold?

◇ security（adv.）警衛

（1）be dedicated to... 奉獻……；致力……（2段）

He would go to a rural part of Hsinchu County to visit children's center dedicated to caring for kids from families hit by unexpected misfortunes.

他會去新竹縣鄉下的一個專門收容家遭變故孩子的兒童中心。

解析

也許讀者會發現原譯文裡的 dedicated to 前面怎麼 BE 動詞不見了。其實它是隱身起來了，我們現在就把它召回：

He would go to a rural part of Hsinchu County to visit a children's center（which was）dedicated to caring for kids from families hit by unexpected misfortunes.

由此可見，關係代名詞（在上句中為 which）的後面為 BE 動詞和過去分詞時，這個關係代名詞和 BE 動詞（在上句中為 was）是可以一起省略的。

小試身手

1. 他們一輩子致力反戰運動。

_____

（2）cannot help Ving... 不禁……；忍不住……；不由得……（5段）

I couldn't help thinking of the kids at that children's center.

我不禁想起那所兒童中心的孩子們。

解析

在這兒，讀者們可不要先入為主地把 help 解釋成「幫忙；援助」。其實它在這裡傾向於 resist「抵擋；擋住」之意。所以除了如句型裡的 cannot help

Ving，你當然也可以使用 cannot resist Ving 來傳達相同的意思。

小試身手

2. 我忍不住偷瞄了坐在走道對面的那個傢伙一眼。

_____

(3) remind 某人of 某事 ……提醒某人某事；令某人想起某事（6 段）

This once again reminded me of New Year's dinner.
這又一次提醒我年夜飯的事。

解析

這種表示法對以中文為母語的人是要花點時間去適應，關鍵在我們比較不習慣那個介詞（在原句中為 of）。在英文裡它卻屢見不鮮。例如：He **informed** me **of** the time and place of the meeting. 有時候使用 of 以外的介詞，那就要更加小心以對了，試看下句：I tried hard to **acquaint** him with **our** native customs.

小試身手

3. 那個味道使我想起媽媽做的家常菜。

_____

(4) as... as can be 非常之……；……不得了；……得很(7段)

Passing by the No. 2 Reception Center, however, I discovered the restaurant inside was as bustling as could be.

路過第二招待所，卻發現裡面的餐廳熱鬧得很。

解析

對照原譯文，譯者利用這個句型來詮釋「無比的……」真是無比的貼切。夏天到深山溪澗裡泡泡水，真是沁涼得很（涼得不得了），不就可以說成 The water in the stream is as cold as can be. 到朋友家作客，朋友的父母直把你當成是自己兒女看待，慈祥和藹之至，銘感在心，不妨就在你的英文日記裡寫下：My friend's parents were as gracious as could be.

小試身手

4. 一看到男友出現，她怒氣全消，溫馴得不得了。

_____

(5) upon closer inspection... 走近一看(7段)

Upon closer inspection, I found that Nun Xu from the children's center I mentioned was chaperoning a group of children inside watching TV.

再一看，我所說的那所兒童中心的徐修女帶著一大批孩子在裡面看電視。

解析

比較級形容詞 closer 在這裡為「更仔細」、「更詳細」的意思，關鍵在介詞 upon，它在這裡的意思趨近於「一……就……」的意味，所以這個用法基本的意思為「更詳細一察看就……」。含羞草一被碰觸就伏倒，英文可以說：The mimosa falls flat on the ground upon the slightest touch.

5. 走近一看，這表面並沒有很光滑。

＿＿＿＿＿＿＿＿＿＿＿＿＿＿＿＿＿＿＿＿＿＿＿＿＿

(6) feel deliciously warm 覺得溫馨；感到暖洋洋的（9段）

I felt deliciously warm inside.

我心裡感到無比的溫暖。

解析

在身體極度疲困，力虛氣弱的時候，尤其是在嚴冬，來一碗溫熱的湯，可口的滋味，加上口腹中的那股暖意，不也曾讓你感到萬般美好嗎？而今有人在你困頓不濟時施恩與你，你會不會也領略到同樣那股如寒天飲熱湯，直上心頭那股可口美好（deliciously）而又暖洋洋（warm）的感覺呢？

6. 讀著信，當看到他安慰的話語時我（心裡）覺得暖洋洋的。

＿＿＿＿＿＿＿＿＿＿＿＿＿＿＿＿＿＿＿＿＿＿＿＿＿

小試身手解答

1. They have dedicated their whole lives to opposing war.

2. I couldn't resist stealing a look at the guy sitting across the aisle.

3. The aroma reminded me of my mother's home cooking.

4. The moment she saw her boyfriend coming, she became as tame as could be, her anger all gone.

5. The surface is not so smooth upon closer inspection.

6. Reading the letter, I felt deliciously warm when my eyes fell on his words of comforting solace.

The Perfect Day

十全十美的一天

1-5　　今天早上，我感到特別的爽。

　　我的五十肩，已經伴隨我快五年了，每天早上醒來，第一個感覺就是左手臂隱隱作痛，可是今天，一點感覺都沒有了。

　　窗外，天特別的藍。微風吹進來，還帶一些桂花的香味。我的枕邊人，卻不見了。原來她在替我做早飯。結婚以後，我就告訴我老婆，人家貴為英國首相的柴契爾夫人，都會替她老公每天早上做早飯，妳也應該如此。我老婆一口拒絕，她說：「早上睡早覺是神聖不可侵犯的人權，早飯你只好自理了。可是如果你做成了英國首相，我願意替你每天做早飯。」這是什麼邏輯？今天，她卻一反常態，在問我：「老公，你要吃炒蛋，還是荷包蛋？」

　　上班了，我照樣偷偷地看報，那位可惡的科長走進來看到我在看報，竟然一句話也不說，還和我聊了幾句。

　　業務會報，我照例亂講一氣，科長聽了以後，居然無所謂的樣子，可是我的那些同事全被他罵得狗血淋頭。

CD2-4　◇ remarkably (adv.) 非常地……；……得不得了
◇ fragrance (n.) 芳香；香氣

1-5

CD2-3

This morning I felt like a million dollars.

I've been plagued with frozen shoulder for nearly five years now. Every morning when I wake up, my first sensation is a dull pain in my left arm. Today, however, I felt no sensation at all.

Outside the window, the sky was remarkably blue. A gentle breeze blew in, carrying with it the fragrance of laurel blossoms. My bedside companion had disappeared, though— as it turned out, she had gone to fix breakfast for me. After I got married, I told my wife that even Margaret Thatcher, the venerable British prime minister, made breakfast for her husband every morning, so she ought to do the same. But my wife flatly refused. She said, "A good morning's sleep is a sacred and inviolable human right. You'll have to take care of breakfast on your own. But if you ever become prime minister of England, I'll make you breakfast every morning." What kind of logic is that? But today she was completely out of character: "Honey, do you want fried eggs or poached?" she asked.

At work, as I snuck my customary peek at the newspaper, that nasty department head walked in, but he didn't say so much as a word of rebuke! He even made a bit of small talk with me.

For my work report, as usual I said whatever nonsense popped into my head, but he didn't seem to mind. My coworkers, on the other hand, he castigated mercilessly.

◇ venerable（adj.）值得尊敬的；令人肅然起敬的
◇ inviolable（adj.）不可侵犯的
◇ nasty（adj.）討厭的；令人痛恨的
◇ castigate（v.）痛罵；厲斥

6-10　　吃午飯的時候，更怪的事發生了，別人的菜都一模一樣地用大鍋菜燒出來的，我卻有一盤回鍋肉，味道也完全對我的胃口，哪有這麼巧？

　　我實在忍不住了，正好隔壁的老王是我的知己，因此我就問他，「老兄，怎麼回事？為什麼我今天什麼事都順利得不得了？」

　　老王反問我：「你真的不知道？」

　　「我真的不知道。」

　　「要知道真相嗎？」

11-15　　「我當然要。」

　　「那就告訴你吧，你已經死了。您應該知道，只有死人才會有這種十全十美的日子。」

　　我大聲抗議：「你胡說，你胡說，我活得好好的……」

　　「老公，你怎麼又講夢話了？」我被我的老婆推醒。「真討厭，一大早講夢話，害得我被你吵醒了。」

◇ identical (adj.) 相同的；一樣的　　◇ coincidence [ko`ɪnsədəns] (n.) 巧合

◇ appetite [`æpə͵taɪt] (n.) 口味；胃口　　◇ smoothly (adv.) 順利地

At lunchtime an even stranger thing happened: everyone else ate identical food that all came from the same big pot, but I got a plate of double-cooked pork, and the taste suited my appetite perfectly. Surely it wasn't just a coincidence?

6-10

I really couldn't take it anymore. My good friend Old Wang happened to be by my side, so I asked him, "Brother, what's going on? Why is everything going so unbelievably smoothly for me today?"

Old Wang replied, "You really don't know?"

"I really don't know."

"Do you want to know the truth?"

"Of course I do."

11-15

"Then I'll tell you: you're dead. You ought to know— only the dead have such completely perfect days."

I loudly protested: "No way, you're making this up. I'm alive and well..."

"Husband, are you talking in your sleep *again*?" I was jolted awake by my wife. "So obnoxious! Talking in your sleep at the crack of dawn, waking me up from a good night's sleep..."

◇ protest (v.) 抗議　　　　　　◇ jolt (v.)（用力）推；搖

我揉了一下眼睛，立刻感到我的肩膀隱隱作痛，我的黃臉婆蓬頭散髮地睡在我旁邊，我忽然覺得她好可愛，忍不住去親了她一下。

16-18　「你瘋了，老瘋子。」這下子她真醒了，立刻下達命令：「下班以後，買一斤里肌肉，我還要一些番茄⋯⋯」

她還在下命令的時候，我早就溜了出來。我知道她的脾氣。只要我記得一兩件東西，帶回家亮相，就可以交差，反正她是個寬宏大量的人。

外面下著大雨，沒有柴契爾夫人替我燒早飯，我只好撐著傘，先去門口小店吃燒餅油條，然後在雨中擠上了公車上班。

上班的時候，我老是笑嘻嘻地。中什，老王對我說：「老李，你吃錯了什麼藥？平常只聽到你發牢騷，是個牢騷大王，今天怎麼一句埋怨的話都沒有了？」我說：「老王，發什麼牢騷？如果你一早醒來，

◇ disheveled（adj.）披頭散髮的；衣衫不整的
◇ lunatic（n.）瘋子；精神不正常的人（註：原譯文 You old lunatic! 大約相當於中文的「老番癲」）

I rubbed my eyes a little and immediately felt a dull pain in my shoulder. My old lady was sleeping all disheveled by my side. Suddenly I thought how cute she looked, and I couldn't resist giving her a kiss.

"You're crazy, you old lunatic." Now she was really awake, and she immediately began issuing orders: "After you get off work, buy a catty of tenderloin. I want some tomatoes, too..."

16-18

While she was still giving orders, I had already slipped out. I know her temperament: as long as I remember to bring home a couple things to keep up appearances, I can say I've fulfilled my duty. In any case, she's a charitable person.

It was raining hard outside, and there was no Mrs. Thatcher to make me breakfast. I could only open up my umbrella, drop by the little shop near the gate for a sesame seed cake and a fried breadstick, then crowd into the bus to go to work.

At work I was in continually high spirits. At lunch, Old Wang said to me, "Old Lee, what's gotten into you? Usually I just hear you complain— you're the master of complaining. How is it I haven't heard you carping about a single thing today?" "Old Wang, what is there to complain about?" I said. "If you woke up one morning and

---

◇ slip (out) (v.) (偷偷地) 溜 (出去)
◇ fulfill (v.) 實現；完成

◇ charitable (adj.) 善心的；慈悲為懷的；急公好義的
◇ carp (v.) 埋怨；碎碎唸

發現世界美得不得了，一點牢騷都沒有，那你就完了。」老王太年輕，他似乎聽不懂我的意思。

discovered how amazingly beautiful the world is— absolutely nothing to complain about— then that'd be the end of you." Old Wang must be too young— he didn't seem to understand what I meant.

◇ amazingly（adv.）令人驚異稱奇地；令人感到不可思議地

(1) feel like a million dollars 心情愉悅；爽快之至（1段）

This morning I felt like a million dollars.

今天早上，我感到特別的爽。

解析

近些年來台灣瘋樂透，市井小民，不參與其中的絕少，當然能一圓發財夢的還是只有那幾位幸運兒。大多數的樂透迷仍是每期槓龜，把中獎的美夢寄託在下一期。如果真讓你中了大獎，百萬千萬甚或億元台幣入袋，你當然樂不可支，「爽」之又「爽」。所以，feel like a million dollars 用來表示「心情愉悅」、「爽快之至」誰曰不宜？

小試身手

1. 我是優勝者的這個宣布讓我覺得非常非常高興。

_____

(2) be plagued with 為……所苦（2段）

I have been plagued with frozen shoulder for nearly five years now.

我的五十肩，已經伴隨我快五年了。

解析

plague 為名詞時，作「瘟疫」解，中古時期的歐洲人聞「鼠疫」（黑死病）而色變，所以，plague 也可以作「鼠疫」解。當然，在這個句型，be plagued 已經是動詞的用法，要把它當成「為……所苦」、「為……所折磨」來看。試想得了瘟疫這種狠毒可怕的流行病，豈不令人痛苦不堪嗎？

2. 這可憐的媽媽為她孩子們的不良行為所苦。

_____

(3) As it turns（turned）out 結果（是）……；原來是……（3段）

My bedside companion had disappeared, though— as it turned out, she had gone to fix breakfast for me.

我的枕邊人，卻不見了。原來她在替我做早飯。

解析

別忘了，turn 這個字的本義為「轉變」、「演變」。某件事情從無到有，從有到結束，總有個由始至終的一個轉變的歷程，用 turn out 來表示「事情演變到最後如何如何」真是很有道理的。有時候英文裡我們用 end up 以表示相同的含意。換個方式來說，原句就可以改寫如下：...she ended up fixing breakfast for me in the kitchen... 或 She ended up in the kitchen fixing breakfast for me.

3. 原來他是那樁駭人罪行的幕後主腦人物。

_____

（4）out of character 非其本性；有違常態；不合常情（3段）

But today she was completely out of character...

今天，她卻一反常態。

解析

看看以下的片語同時揣摩它們的意思：out of work / out of order / out of breath / out of mind / out of control / out of debt……怎樣，有心得嗎？沒錯 out of work 是「失業」、「沒頭路」；out of order 是「失序」、「故障」；out of breath 是「喘不過氣」、「上氣不接下氣」；out of mind 是「發瘋」、「精神失常」；out of control 是「失控」、「不正常」；out of debt 是「沒有債務」、「債務還清」。從以下這些片語，你當然看得出來，out of 有濃濃的「失去……」、「跳脫……」的味道。所以不妨想想看：out of 後面跟著 character 會產生什麼效應？對了，那當然就是「非其本性」、「一反常態」、「不合常理常情」的意思囉。

小試身手

4. 她一反常態，坐著而沒有發表任何評論。

　　_____

（5）say whatever（nonsense）pop into one's head 想到什麼說什麼（5段）

For my work report, as usual I said whatever nonsense popped into my head, but he didn't seem to mind.

業務會報，我照例亂講一氣，科長聽了以後，居然無所謂的樣子。

解析

吃過爆米花吧，看過爆米花在機器裡噼哩啪啦（pop）作響，上下左右彈跳吧，也難怪爆米花就叫作 popcorn（pop + corn）了。因此，心裡突發奇想，

有個什麼念頭突然閃進腦海（就像爆米花啪一聲蹦進腦海），英文就說 pop into one's head，你說妙不妙？

小試身手

5. 我起先是智盡才竭，後來突然一個念頭閃進腦海，我決定它可以一試。

_____

---

(6) 幾個重要口語用法（13段）

I loudly protested: "No way, you're making this up. I'm alive and well..."

我大聲抗議：「你胡說，你胡說，我活得好好的……」

解析

No way. 表示「絕無此事」、「根本沒有的事」；You're making this up. 則表示「你在編故事騙人」、「你在瞎說胡扯」；至於 alive 表示「活著」而 well 意指「健康」，所以 alive and well 大約和中文說「健在」一般意思。

小試身手

6. 他鼓勵我說實話而不要隨便亂說。

_____

（7） **What's gotten into you**（me, him, her,...）**?**（某人）是怎麼了？
（某人）有什麼不對勁的？（某人）吃錯了什麼藥？

"Old Lee, what's gotten into you?"
老李，你吃錯了什麼藥？

解析

這句話意思雖然和 What's wrong with you? What's the matter with you? 相去不遠，但是想必讀者都可以感受到這句話的活潑自然。動詞用 get into，和中文用「中了（什麼）邪」、「著了（什麼）道」表示某人言行舉止不正常，一樣白話而又通俗的口吻，是一句很道地，很直接的口語英文，豈容放過？

小試身手

7. 我也搞不清楚我今天是那根筋不對勁。

＿＿＿＿＿＿＿＿＿＿＿＿＿＿＿＿＿＿＿＿＿

（8） **the master of complaining** 最會（發牢騷）；（牢騷）大王

Usually I just hear you complain— you're the master of complaining.
平常只聽到你發牢騷，是個牢騷大王。

解析

master 原是「巨匠」、「宗師」這樣的道行高超、技藝出類拔萃的人物。在某一行的修煉和功力都已達爐火純青，非一般人所能企及的境界，發牢騷的功力臻此，豈可不尊之為王呢？

也作 a master，但用 the master 更是強調真的沒有人可以比得上。

小試身手

8. 何不和她去購物？她最會討價還價了。

_____

小試身手解答

1. The announcement that I was the winner made me feel like a million dollars.

2. The poor mother is plagued by her children's problematic behavior.

3. As it turned out, he was the mastermind behind the hideous crime.

4. It was quite out of character for her to remain seated without making any criticisms.

5. Originally I was at my wits' end, but then an idea popped into my head and I decided it was worth a try.

6. He encouraged me to tell the truth instead of making things up.

7. I don't know what's gotten into me either.

8. Why not go shopping with her? She's a master of haggling prices.

Let the Wall Fall:
— Reflections on meeting Mother Teresa

讓高牆倒下吧
——訪問德蕾莎修女的感想

1-5　　　　五十年前，一群來自歐洲的天主教修女們住在印度的加爾各答，她們住在一所宏偉的修道院內，雖然生活很有規律，可是一般說來，她們的生活是相當安定而且舒適的，修道院建築以外還有整理得非常漂亮的花園，花園裡的草地更是綠草如茵。

　　　　整個修道院四面都有高牆，修女們是不能隨意走出高牆的，有時為了看病，才會出去。可是她們都會乘汽車去，而且也會立刻回來。

　　　　高牆內，生活舒適而安定，圍牆外，卻是完全一個不同的世界。二次世界大戰爆發，糧食運輸因為軍隊的運輸而受了極大的影響，物價大漲，大批農人本來就沒有多少儲蓄，現在這些儲蓄因為通貨膨脹而化為烏有，因此加爾各答城裡湧入了成千上萬的窮人，據說大約有兩百萬人因此而餓死。沒有餓死的人也只有住在街上，一直到今天，我們都可以看到這些住在街上的人，過著非常悲慘的生活。舉個例來說，我曾在加爾各答的街道上，親眼看到一個小孩子，用一只杯子在陰溝裡盛水洗臉，漱口，最後索性盛了一大杯，痛痛快快地將水喝了下去。

CD2-12　◇ magnificent（adj.）富麗堂皇的　　　◇ surround（v.）環繞；圍繞
　　　　◇ meticulously（adv.）細心地；煞費苦心地　◇ secure（adj.）安全的；穩固的

1-5

Fifty years ago, a group of European Catholic nuns lived in Calcutta, India. They lived in a magnificent convent, and though there were many rules they had to obey, on the whole they lived lives of comfort and ease. Outside the convent, there was a meticulously tended flower garden with fields of soft green grass.

The convent was surrounded by high walls, and the nuns could not go outside the walls without some special reason. Occasionally they would get sick and have to go see a doctor, but on those occasions they traveled by car, and they would return immediately afterward.

Within the walls, life was comfortable and secure, but outside them, it was an entirely different world. World War II broke out, and the transport of soldiers had a huge adverse impact on the transport of food. Prices skyrocketed. Multitudes of farmers had had but little savings to begin with, and now what little they did have vanished with inflation. As a result, thousands upon thousands of poor people streamed into Calcutta, and it is said that two million starved to death. Those who survived the famine were forced to live on the streets; to this day, one can still see these street-dwellers living out their tragic lives. For example, one time I saw a small child scooping water from the gutter. First he washed his face, then he rinsed out his mouth, and finally he filled a big cupful and gulped it down heartily.

◇ transport (n.) 運輸；輸送　　　　　　◇ vanish (v.) 消失不見

　　就在我旅館門口，兩個小男孩每天晚上會躺下睡覺，他們合蓋一塊布，哥哥最多只有三歲大，弟弟恐怕只有三歲不到，兩人永遠佔據同一個地方，也永遠幾乎相擁在一起，他們十一點準時睡覺，早上六時以後就不見蹤影了。

　　這些孩子，很多終其一生沒有能夠走進任何一個房子，也可能終身沒有嚐過自來水的滋味。

6-10　　住在修道院的修女們知道外面的悲慘世界嗎？這永遠是個謎，可是對這些來自歐洲的修女們，印度是一個落後的國家，這種悲慘情景不算什麼特別，她們的任務只是辦好一所貴族化的女子學校，教好一批有錢家庭的子女們。

　　德蕾莎修女就在這座高牆之內，她出身於一個有良好教養的南斯拉夫家庭，從小受到天主教的教育，十八歲進了這所修道院，成為一位修女，雖然她已來到了印度，她的生活仍然很歐洲式的。

　　可是有一次到大吉嶺隱休的途中，德蕾莎修女感到天主給她一道命令，她應該為世上最窮的人服務。

◇ quilt(n.)蓋被
◇ huddle(together)(v.)擠(在一起)；瑟縮(在一堆)
◇ promptly(adv.)準時地
◇ running water(n.)自來水
◇ wretchedness(n.)悲慘；痛苦

At the entrance of my hotel, two boys lied down to sleep each night, sharing a single piece of cloth as a quilt. The bigger one could not have been more than three years old, and the smaller one was younger still. The two of them always occupied the same spot, and were almost always huddled together. They would go to sleep promptly at 11, and after 6 in the morning there would be no trace of them.

Many of these children go through their whole lives without ever once being able to enter a house of any kind, and possibly without ever knowing the taste of running water.

6-10

Did the nuns inside the convent know about the world of wretchedness outside? That will always remain a mystery. But in the eyes of these European nuns, India was a backward country— such scenes of misery were nothing out of the ordinary. Their job was to run an elite girls' school to educate the offspring of rich families.

It was within these walls that Mother Teresa lived. She had grown up in a respectable family in Yugoslavia, where she had received a Catholic education from an early age. At eighteen, she entered the Calcutta convent and became a nun. Although she had come to India, her mode of living was still European.

But one day, as she was on her way to seek spiritual seclusion in Darjeeling, Mother Teresa felt the Lord give her a commandment: she ought to serve the poorest of the world's poor.

◇ mystery (n.) 奧秘；難解之謎
◇ backward (adj.) 落伍的
◇ elite [eˋlit] (n.) 菁英份子，貴族
◇ respectable family (n.) 望族
◇ mode of living (n.) 生活方式
◇ spiritual seclusion (n.) 閉關靈修

一九四八年，德蕾莎修女離開了她住了二十多年的修道院，她脫下了那套厚重的黑色歐洲式修女道袍，換上了一件像印度農婦穿的白色衣服，這套衣服有藍色的邊，德蕾莎修女從此要走出高牆，走入一個貧窮、髒亂的悲慘世界。

高牆到今天都仍存在，可是對德蕾莎修女而言，高牆消失了，她從此不再過舒適而安定的生活，她每天看到有人赤身露體的躺在街上，也不能忽視很多人躺在路上奄奄一息，即將去世。她更不能假裝看不到有人的膀子被老鼠咬掉了一大片。下身也幾乎完全被蟲吃掉。

德蕾莎修女是一個人走出去的，她要直接替最窮的人服務。即使對天主教會而言，這仍是怪事，很多神父認為她大錯特錯，可是她的信仰一直支持著她，使她在遭遇多少挫折之後仍不氣餒。

11-15　　到今天，四十六年以後，德蕾莎修女已是家喻戶曉的人物。今年十一月十六日，她將來靜宜大學接受榮譽博士學位，為了增加對她的瞭解，我決定親自到加爾各答看她。

◇ habit (n.)（修行人士所穿的）僧衣；道袍
◇ filthiness (n.) 骯髒；污穢
◇ exist (v.) 存在
◇ naked [`nekɪd] (adj.) 赤身露體的；沒穿衣服的
◇ ignore (v.) 對……視而不見；無視

In 1948, Mother Teresa left the convent that had been her home for more than twenty years. She took off her thick, heavy European-style black habit and exchanged it for a light white garment with blue trim, similar to what Indian farm women wear. At that moment, Mother Teresa walked outside of the wall and into a world of poverty, filthiness and misery.

The wall still stands today, but for Mother Teresa, from then on it no longer existed. Never again would she live in comfort and ease. Every day she would see people lying naked in the streets. She couldn't ignore the many people lying in the road gasping for air, on the verge of death, nor could she pretend not to see how rats had eaten away a big chunk of a man's arm, or how his lower half, too, had been almost completely devoured by vermin.

Mother Teresa went out alone, resolved to directly serve the poorest of the poor. This was eccentric even in the eyes of the Catholic church— a lot of priests thought she was gravely misguided— but her faith continually supported her, enabling her to keep her chin up no matter how hard things got.

Now, forty-six years later, Mother Teresa has become a household name. On November 16 of this year, she will come to Providence University to accept an honorary doctorate degree. In order to understand her better, I decided to personally visit her in Calcutta.

11-15

◇ pretend (v.) 佯裝；假裝
◇ devour (v.) 吞噬；（大口）吃掉；吞下
◇ eccentric (adj.) 怪異的；古怪的
◇ church (n.) 教會
◇ gravely (adv.) 嚴重地
◇ honorary doctorate degree 榮譽博士學位

我們了解的德蕾莎修女

德蕾莎修女究竟是一個什麼樣的人？

她的第一個特徵是絕對的貧窮，她不僅為最窮的人服務而已，她還要求自己也成為窮人，她只有三套衣服，她不穿襪子，只穿涼鞋，她的住處除了電燈以外，唯一的電氣用具是電話，這還是最近才裝的。電腦等一概沒有。

她也沒有秘書替她安排時間，沒有秘書替她回信，信都由她親筆回，在我去訪問她以前，中山大學的楊昌彪教授說她一定會有一群公關人員，替她做宣傳，否則她如何會如此有名？而且怎麼會有這麼多人跟隨她，我覺得這好像有些道理，我想如果她有這麼一位公關人員，我可以向她要一套介紹德蕾莎修女的錄影帶，可是我錯了，她沒有任何公關人員，更沒有任何宣傳品。

◇ characteristic(n.)特徵；特質；特色
◇ set(n.)組；套(註：一套工具：a set of tools；一組齊全的餐具：a full set of tableware)

The Mother Teresa we know

CD2-6

Just what kind of person is Mother Teresa?

Her first characteristic is absolute poverty. She does not merely serve the poor— she requires herself to become one of them. She has only three sets of clothes, and she doesn't wear socks, only sandals. In her home, the only electric appliance besides the light is a telephone, and it was only recently that she installed it. There is nothing remotely resembling a computer.

She has no secretary to arrange her schedule, nor does she have one to answer her mail— she replies to each of her letters with her own pen. Before I went to interview her, Professor C. B. Yang of Sun Yat-sen University said that she must have a public relations team to publicize her work— otherwise, how could she have gotten so famous? And how could she have attracted so many followers? I thought that seemed to make sense. If she had a PR chief, I thought, then I could ask her for a videotape introducing her work. But I was wrong— she has no PR team, and she has no propaganda.

◇ electric appliance (n.) 電器
◇ install (v.) 安裝；裝設
◇ resemble (v.) 相似；像

◇ public relations team (n.) 公關小組
◇ propaganda (n.) 宣傳

在天主教各個修會人數往下降的時候，她的修會卻一直蓬勃發展，現在已有七千多位修女和修士們參加了這個仁愛修會。修士修女們宣誓終其一生要全心全意地為「最窮」的人服務。

16-20　　至於她的思想呢？

德蕾莎修女常常強調耶穌在十字架臨死的一句話「我渴」，對德蕾莎修女而言，耶穌當時代表了古往今來全人類中所有受苦受難的人。所謂渴不僅是生理上的需要水喝，而且也代表在受苦受難時最需要的是來自人類的愛，來自人類的關懷。

德蕾莎修女成立了一百多個替窮人服務的處所，每個處所都有耶穌被釘在十字架上的苦像，而在十字架旁邊，都有「我渴」這兩個字。她要提醒大家，任何一個人在痛苦中，我們就應在他的身上看到基督的影子，任何替這不幸的人所做的，都是替基督所做的。

◇ Catholic monastic order(n.)**天主教修會**　　◇ stress(v.)**強調**

◇ flourish (v.)**滋長茁壯；興盛壯大**　　◇ represent(v.)**意味；象徵；代表**

As membership in every other Catholic monastic order has fallen, hers has continually flourished: currently more than seven thousand nuns and monks are devoted to her charitable order. Her nuns and monks take an oath to spend the rest of their lives in sincere, devoted service to the poorest of the poor.

What about her philosophy?

16-20

Mother Teresa often stresses the words Jesus spoke while dying on the cross: "I thirst." In her view, when He spoke those words, Jesus was speaking for all people who have suffered throughout all ages of the world. This thirst is more than a biological need for water. It represents a sufferer's deepest needs: the need for human love and the need for human fellowship.

Mother Teresa has established over a hundred centers for serving the poor, and at each one there is a picture of Christ suffering on the cross. Beside each cross is written the words, "I thirst." She wishes to remind all of us that we should see the image of Christ in anyone who is suffering. Anything done for an unfortunate soul is something done for Christ Himself.

◇ fellowship (n.) 民吾同胞；四海之內皆　　　◇ cross (n.) 十字架
　兄弟；交誼　　　　　　　　　　　　　　◇ soul (n.) 人（註：一般作「靈魂」解
◇ establish (v.) 成立；建立　　　　　　　　　釋，但在此處作「人」解）

德蕾莎的默想禱文這樣說的：
一顆純潔的心，很容易看到基督
在飢餓的人中
在赤身露體的人中
在無家可歸的人中
在寂寞的人中
在沒有人要的人中
在沒有人愛的人中
在痲瘋病人當中
在酗酒的人中
在躺在街上的乞丐中

窮人餓了，不僅只希望有一塊麵包而已，更希望有人愛他；窮人赤身露體，不僅希望有人給他一塊布，更希望有人能給他應有的尊嚴。

21-25　　窮人無家可歸，不僅希望有一間小屋可以棲身，而且也希望再也沒有人遺棄他、忘了他，對他漠不關心。

德蕾莎修女不只是一位社會工作者而已，為了要服務最窮的人，她的修士修女們都要變成窮人，修士們連手錶都不准戴，只有如此，被修士修女們服務的窮人才會感到有一些尊嚴。

◇ meditation (n.) 冥想；沉思
◇ alcoholic (n.) 酗酒的人
◇ dignity (n.) 尊嚴
◇ deserve (v.) 應得

Teresa's meditation prayer goes like this:

It is easy for a pure heart to see Christ
Among the hungry
Among the naked
Among the homeless
Among the lonely
Among the unwanted
Among the unloved
Among the lepers
Among the alcoholics
Among the beggars lying in the streets

When a poor man is hungry, he doesn't just wish for a piece of bread, but for someone to love him; when a poor man is naked, he doesn't just wish for a piece of clothing, but for someone to give him the dignity he deserves.

When a poor man is homeless, he doesn't just wish for a place to stay, but that no one will ever abandon him, forget him, or be coldly indifferent to him again.

21-25

Mother Teresa is more than a mere social worker. In order to serve the poorest of the poor, her monks and nuns must become poor themselves; the monks aren't even allowed to wear watches. Only thus can the destitute people they serve feel like they have some dignity.

◇ indifferent(adj.)冷漠的；漠不關心的　　◇ destitute(adj.)赤貧的
◇ social worker(n.)社會工作者(社工)

只有親眼看到，才可以體會到這種替窮人服務的精神，他們不只是在「服務」窮人，他們幾乎是在「侍奉」窮人。

德蕾莎修女說她知道她不能解決人類中貧困問題。這個問題，必須留給政治家、科學家，和經濟學家慢慢地解決，可是她等不了，她知道世界上太多人過著毫無尊嚴的非人生活，她必須先照顧他們。

因為修士修女們過著窮人的生活，德蕾莎修女不需大量的金錢，她從不募款，以她的聲望，只要她肯辦一次慈善晚宴，全世界的大公司都會捐錢，可是她永遠不肯。她不願做這類的事情，以確保她的修士修女們的純潔。她們沒有公關單位，顯然也是這個原因。

事實上德蕾莎修女最喜歡的不僅是有人捐錢給她，她更希望有人肯來做義工。

26-30 在德蕾莎修女的默想文中，有一句話是我一直不能瞭解的：

一顆純潔的心

會自由地給

自由地愛

直到它受到創傷

◇ politician (n.) 政治家；政治工作者
◇ economist (n.) 經濟學家
◇ term (n.) 時期；學期；任期
◇ devoid (of) (adj.) 缺乏的

The only way to really feel the spirit of serving poor people like this is to witness it in person. They don't merely provide services for the poor— they really *serve* them.

Mother Teresa says she knows she can't solve the problem of human poverty. That problem must be left to politicians, scientists and economists to solve over the long term. But she can't wait that long. She knows there are too many people in the world whose lives are so devoid of dignity that they are barely human lives at all, and she must take care of them first.

Because her monks and nuns live lives of poverty, Mother Teresa doesn't need a lot of money. She has never gone fundraising, although given her reputation, if she were ever to organize a charity dinner, big corporations all over the world would donate money. But she will never do it. She refuses because she wants to ensure that her monks and nuns stay pure in heart. Her lack of a PR team is obviously another factor.

What Mother Teresa likes best is not when people donate money, but when people come to volunteer.

`CD2-7`

There is a sentence in Mother Teresa's meditation that I never used to understand:

26-30

A pure heart
Will give freely
And love freely
Until it is wounded

◇ fundraising（n.）籌款；募款
◇ reputation（n.）名譽；聲望
◇ organize（v.）籌劃；主辦
◇ donate（v.）捐款
◇ volunteer（v.）當義工；做義工

說實話，我一直不懂，何謂「心靈受傷」。這次去見德蕾莎修女的工作場所，參加了修士修女們的工作，才真正了解所謂「心靈受傷」和愛的關係。

和德蕾莎修女的五分鐘會面

要見德蕾莎修女，只有一個辦法，那就是早上去望六點鐘的彌撒，我和她約好九月四日早上九點見面。五點五十分，我就到了，修女們都已到齊，大家席地而坐，這好像是她的命令，教堂裡沒有跪凳，一方面是省錢，二方面大概是徹底的印度化。除了修女以外，幾十個外國人也在場，後來我才知道這些全是修女的義工，來自全世界。

我到處找，總算找到這個名聞世界的修女，她在最後一排的小角落裡，這個精神領袖一點架子都沒有，靜靜地站在修女們的最後一排。

◇ relationship (n.)關係
◇ attend(v.)參加；出席
◇ assemble(v.)集合；聚集
◇ row(n.)(橫向的)列

To be frank, I never really understood what "wounds of the heart" were. But on this trip to Mother Teresa's workplace, as I took part in the work of her monks and nuns, I finally came to a true understanding of the relationship between "wounds of the heart" and love.

Five minutes with Mother Teresa

There is only one way to meet Mother Teresa, and that is to get up to attend her 6 am Mass. I arranged to meet with her at 9 in the morning on September 4. When I arrived at 5:50, her nuns were already fully assembled. Everyone sat on the ground; this seemed to be a rule of hers, judging by the absence of anything to sit or kneel on, probably to save money on the one hand and to be as Indian as possible on the other. Besides the nuns, quite a few foreigners were there as well, whom I later found out were the nuns' volunteers; they came from all over the world.

I looked all around before I finally found the world-famous nun in a little corner of the back row. There was absolutely no air of pretentiousness about the spiritual leader; she stood quietly at the rear of her nuns.

◇ pretentiousness (n.) 裝模作樣；矯揉做作

　　彌撒完了，一大堆的人要見她，我這才發現，德蕾莎修女沒有會客室，她就赤著腳站在教堂外的走廊上和每一位要和她見面的人談話，這些人沒有一位要求和她合影，雖然每人只談了幾分鐘，輪到我，已經半小時去掉，在我後面，還有二十幾位在等。

31-35　　她居然記得她要去靜宜接受榮譽博士學位。雖然她親口在電話中和我敲定十一月十六日，雖然我寄了三封信給她，告訴她日期已經敲定，可是她仍然忘了是哪一天，所以我面交了最後一封信，信上再次說明是十一月十六日。然後我們又討價還價地講她究竟能在台灣待幾天，她最後同意四天。

　　我問她有沒有拍任何錄影帶描寫她們的工作，她說沒有；我問她有沒有什麼書介紹她的工作，她也說沒有，可是她說附近有一座大教堂，也許我可以在哪裡找到這種書。我沒有問她有沒有公關主任，答案已經很明顯了。

◇ reception room 接待室；招待室　　　　◇ request (v.) 要求

Mass ended, and a horde of people wanted to see her. It was then I noticed that Mother Teresa had no reception room. She simply stood, barefoot, in the hallway outside the chapel and spoke with each person who wanted to meet with her. None of them requested to take a photo with her. Even though each person only talked for a few minutes, by the time my turn came, half an hour had already passed, and more than twenty other people were waiting behind me.

Remarkably, she actually remembered that she would soon be going to Providence to accept her honorary doctorate. Although she had told me over the phone that she would come the sixteenth of November, and although I had sent her three letters telling her the date had been confirmed, she had still managed to forget which day she was coming. So I hand-delivered a final letter which explained once again that the date would be November 16. Then we haggled back and forth about how long she could stay in Taiwan. Eventually she agreed to stay for four days.

31-35

I asked her if she had ever had anything filmed to describe her work; she said no. I asked her if she had any sort of book introducing her work; she again said no, but she did mention that there was a large church in the neighborhood where I might be able to find a book like that. I didn't ask her if she had a PR chief— the answer was already obvious.

◇ confirm (v.) 確認；確定
◇ haggle (back and forth) (v.) 討價還價；砍（價）；殺（價）
◇ obvious (adj.) 一清二楚的；明顯的

　　我想做的事情都沒有做到，因為我給了她一張支票，她要簽收據，折騰了幾分鐘，後面還有二十幾個人，我只好結束了會面，我後面的一位只說了一句話「我從倫敦來的」，一面給她一些現款，一面跪下來親吻修女的腳，她非常不好意思，可是也沒有拒絕。我這才發現，她的腳已因為風濕而變了形。

垂死之家的經驗

　　我在加爾各答可以有三天的自由活動，因此決定去修女創辦的垂死之家做義工。

　　垂死之家，是德蕾莎修女創立的，有次她看到一位流浪漢坐在一棵樹下，已快去世了，她在火車上，無法下來看他，等她再坐火車回來，發現他已去世了。當時她有一個想法，如果有人在他臨走以前和他談談，一定可以使他比較平安地死去。

36-40　　還有一次，德蕾莎修女在街上發現了一位老婦人，她的身體到處都被老鼠和蟲所咬壞。她將她帶到好幾家醫院，雖然有一家醫院終於接受了她，她在幾小時內就去世。

◇ accomplish（v.）完成；達成
◇ receipt（n.）收據

◇ embarrassed（adj.）不好意思的；難為情的

I didn't accomplish a single one of the things I had wanted to do. Since I gave her a check, she had to sign a receipt; things dragged on for several minutes, and as there were still twenty people behind me, I was forced to cut our meeting short. The fellow behind me said only one sentence: "I've come from London." He handed her a cash donation as he knelt to kiss the nun's feet. She was extremely embarrassed, but she did not reject him. It was then I noticed that rheumatism had changed the shape of her feet.

Experiencing the Home for the Dying

I had three days of free time in Calcutta, so I decided to go volunteer at the nuns' Home for the Dying.

The Home for the Dying was founded by Mother Teresa. She once saw a homeless man sitting under a tree, dying. She was on a train at the time, so she couldn't get off to see him. When she took another train back to see him, she found he was already dead. It was then that a thought occurred to her: if someone had talked with him as he was about to leave this world, he would no doubt have passed away more peacefully.

Another time, Mother Teresa discovered an old woman in the street **36-40** whose body had been bitten all over by rats and insects. She took her to several hospitals, and though one hospital eventually took her in, she passed away a few hours later.

◇ insect(n.) 昆蟲

　　德蕾莎因此創立了垂死之家，在這裡的人，必須要病危而且要無家可歸的流浪者。

　　加爾各答滿街都是無家可歸的人，晚上出去必須小心走路，不然一定會碰到睡在地上的人。有一位義工告訴我，有一位愛爾蘭女士，每天在街上走來走去，如果看到有病重的人，就會送到垂死之家去，她也常常發現麻瘋病人。德蕾莎修女和一家救護車行，有一種共識，他們會替她服務，會將這種病人送到修女的麻瘋病院去。

　　在垂死之家，病人有人照顧，即使最後去世，在去世以前，至少感到了人間的溫暖，因為修士修女們都非常地和善，他們盡量地握病人的手，如果病人情形嚴重，一定有人握住他的手，以便讓他感到人類對他的關懷與愛。

　　雖然德蕾莎修女是天主教修女，她絕對尊重別人的宗教，每一位病人去世以後，都會照他的宗教信仰火葬。

41-45　　九月四日，垂死之家的義工奇多，可是每個人都忙得不亦樂乎，我第一件工作是洗衣服，洗了一個小時，我溜到樓上去曬衣服，這才發

◇ specifically（adv.）特別地；專門地
◇ tacit（adj.）不明講的；不說出來的（註：tacit agreement 相當於中文的「默契」）
◇ ambulance（n.）救護車

Thus, Teresa established a Home for the Dying specifically for homeless wanderers who were seriously ill.

The streets of Calcutta are filled with the homeless: one has to tread carefully at night for fear of bumping into someone sleeping on the ground. A volunteer told me of an Irish woman who would walk around the streets each day, and if she saw someone who was very sick, she would take him to the Home for the Dying. She often found lepers, too. Mother Teresa had a tacit agreement with an ambulance service that would help her by taking those people to the nuns' hospital for lepers.

The patients at the Home for the Dying had people to take care of them. Even if in the end they died anyway, at least they would feel some human warmth before death came, for the monks and nuns were very kind. They would always try to hold the patients' hands. If a patient was in critical condition, there would always be someone to hold his hand to let him feel some human affection.

Although Teresa is a Catholic nun, she absolutely respects others' religions. Every time a sick man passes away, he is cremated in accordance with his beliefs.

CD2-8

On September 4 there was a particularly large number of volunteers, but they were all happily busy. My first task was washing clothes; after washing for an hour, I wandered upstairs to hang the

41-45

◇ critical (adj.) 危急的；嚴重的（註：in critical condition 相當於中文「病情告急」、「病危」）

◇ human affection 人性溫暖；人性關懷

◇ cremate [ˋkrimet] (v.) (屍體) 火化

現他們連夾衣服的夾子都沒有。正好碰到大風，只好每件衣服都打個結。

曬衣服回來，忽然有人叫我：「修士，有人去世，你要來幫忙抬遺體，」我不是修士，可是也不敢否認，因此我就去抬了，抬入一間暫停的停屍間。我沒有看到她什麼樣子，只感到她的遺體輕得出奇。

快十一點了，一位神父來做彌撒，經文用英文，可是所有的聖歌都是用印度文的，極像佛教僧侶的吟唱，只是更有活力，調子也快得多，除了風琴之外，還有一位男修士在打鼓，這些男修士唱歌的時候，活像美國黑人唱靈歌一樣地陶醉，很多修女在彌撒時繼續工作，只有領聖時候才前去領聖體。彌撒完了，我們要分送飯，我發現病人們吃的還不錯，是咖哩肉飯。在這以前，我注意到一個青年的病人，頂多十五歲，他曾經叫我替他弄一杯牛奶喝，我也一匙一匙地餵他，現在他又要我餵他吃。一位修女說我慣壞了他，因為他一向都是自己吃的。修女說顯然他很喜歡我，吃完了飯，他還拉著我的手不放。

◇ knot（n.）結（註：tie a knot 相當於中文「打個結」）

◇ morgue [mɔrg]（n.）太平間；停屍處
◇ light（adj.）輕的

clothes out to dry, only to discover that there were no clothespins. It happened to be quite windy at the time, so I was forced to tie a knot in each piece of clothing.

As I came back from drying clothes, suddenly someone called to me, "Brother, someone's passed away. Come help move the body." I was not a monk, but I didn't dare refuse, so off I went to lift the body and carry it into a morgue. I didn't see what she looked like— I only felt that her body was remarkably light.

Shortly before eleven, a priest came to offer Mass. The scriptures were in English, but all the hymns were in Hindi; they sounded just like Buddhist monks chanting, only livelier and at a much faster tempo. Besides an organist, there was also a monk playing the drums. Like African-Americans singing spirituals, these monks were totally absorbed in their music. Many nuns kept working during Mass, stopping only to take communion when it was offered. Mass ended, and it was time to deliver meals. I found that the patients' food was really not bad: it was curry meat with rice. Before this, a young patient, no more than fifteen, had caught my eye. He had asked me to make him a cup of milk, and I had fed it to him spoonful by spoonful. Now he wanted me to feed him again. A nun said that I'd spoiled him— he'd always eaten by himself before. She said he must really like me. After he finished eating, he took hold of my hand and wouldn't let go.

◇ chant (v.) (詩歌；宗教經文) 吟唱；吟誦　　◇ absorbed (in) (adj.) 聚精會神；專心一意
◇ tempo (n.) 節奏；節拍　　◇ let go 放手；放開

　　快到十二點的時候，一個傢伙來找我，「修士，那位病人要上廁所，」我這才知道，這位年輕病人已弱得不能走路，我扶著他慢慢走去，發現他好矮。他上廁所的時候完全要我扶著，這裡是沒有馬桶的。

　　義工哪裡來的？做什麼事？絕大多數的義工來自歐洲，也有來自日本和新加坡的，我沒有碰到來自美國的義工，也只見到一位印度義工，而且是從歐洲回來的。其他一半義工大概是在學的學生，暑假全泡在這裡了，另一半大都是已就業的人士。令我感到吃驚的是很多醫生來了，我就碰到六位，都來自歐洲。還有一位是義大利的銀行家，雖然他不講，也看得出來，他每年必來，一來起碼兩個星期。年輕的義工常常在此工作三個月之久。

46-50　　義工無貴賤，聽說過去曾有美國加州州長在此服務過一個月，修女們假裝不認識他，他的工作也和大家一樣。

　　第二天，我發現我的工作更多了，第一件是洗碗，用的清潔劑是石灰，看起來好髒，病人的碗都是不鏽鋼的，不怕這種粗糙的石灰。不

◇ toilet(n.)馬桶
◇ majority(n.)大多數
◇ previously(adv.)之前地；以前地
◇ employ (v.)僱用；聘請

At almost noon, a fellow came looking for me: "Brother, that sick boy needs to use the bathroom." Only then did I find out that the boy was too weak to walk. Supporting him with my body, I walked slowly there, noticing how short he was. When he did his business, he relied completely on me to hold him up— there was no toilet to sit on.

Where did the volunteers come from? What did they do for a living? The vast majority were from Europe, while others hailed from Japan and Singapore; I didn't meet any American volunteers. I only saw one Indian, and he had previously lived in Europe. Half the volunteers were students still in school; they spent their entire summer vacations there. Most of the other half were employed. What surprised me was how many doctors there were: I met six, all of whom were European. There was also an Italian banker who, although he didn't say so, looked as if he came every year and stayed for at least two weeks each time. The younger volunteers often worked there for three months straight.

Among the volunteers, there is no distinction between rich and poor. I heard that a former governor of California once served here for a month, but the nuns pretended not to recognize him, and his work was the same as everyone else's.

46-50

On my second day I found I had even more work to do than before. My first job was washing dishes with filthy-looking lime for dish

◇ straight(adv.)接續地；連續地（註：for three months straight為「接連三個月」之意）

◇ distinction(n.)分野；不同

◇ governor(n.)州長

◇ recognize(v.)認得；認出

過水很快就變成黑水。第二件工作是替洗好澡的病人穿衣服,我這才發現病人有多瘦,瘦得像從納粹集中營裡放出來的,似乎一點肉都沒有了。

在任何時刻,病人都會要水喝,我們義工不停地給他們水喝,有時也要給他們沖牛奶,有一位病人最為麻煩,他一開始認為我不該給他冷牛奶,我只好去找熱水。廚房的廚娘不是修女,兇得要命,用印度話把我臭罵,我不懂我做錯了什麼,只好求救於一位修女。後來才知道,我不該將病人用的杯子靠近燒飯的地方。好不容易加了熱水,他又嫌太燙,我加了冷水,他又說怎麼沒有糖,好在我知道糖在哪裡,加了糖以後,他總算滿意了,也謝了我,而且叫我好孩子。我在想,這位老先生一定很有錢,過去每天在家使喚佣人,現在被人家遺棄,積習仍未改,可是因為我們要侍奉窮人,也就只好聽由他使喚了。

◇ stainless steel 不銹鋼
◇ emaciated [ɪˈmeʃɪ̩etɪd](adj.)（因病而）消瘦的；孱弱的
◇ liberated（adj.)釋放；解脫
◇ Nazi concentration camp 納粹集中營
◇ muscle(n.)肌肉

soap. All the patients' bowls were made of stainless steel that the rough lime could not damage, but the water soon became black. My second task was to help dress the patients after they bathed. This was the first time I saw just how skinny they were, as emaciated as prisoners freshly liberated from a Nazi concentration camp, seemingly without any muscle at all.

At any given time, a patient might ask for a drink of water, so we volunteers were constantly supplying water for them. Sometimes we would have to mix them powdered milk as well. One sick man was particularly bothersome: he thought I shouldn't have given him cold milk, so I had to go look for hot water. The kitchen worker I met, who was not a nun, was as mean as a junkyard dog: she cursed me out in Hindi. I didn't understand what I had done wrong, so I went to a nun for help. From her I learned that I shouldn't bring the patients' cups anywhere near the kitchen. When I finally got some hot water, he complained it was too hot; when I added cold water, he asked why there was no sugar. Luckily I knew where the sugar was; after I had added some, he was finally satisfied. He even thanked me, calling me a good boy. I figured this old man must once have been rich, accustomed to ordering servants around, and though he was now abandoned, his old habits were hard to break. But because we were there to serve the poor, we had no choice but to let him order us around.

◇ powdered milk 奶粉

◇ bothersome (adj.) 煩人的；騷擾的

◇ curse (v.) (尤指用髒話或粗話) 罵

◇ accustomed (to) (adj.) 習慣的；習以為常的

◇ abandon (v.) 拋棄不顧；棄之不理

　　第三件工作是洗衣服，無聊之至。洗衣中，又有人叫我修士，要我送藥給病人，我高興極了，因為這件事輕鬆而愉快，有一位青年的修士負責配藥，配完之後，我們給一位一位病人送去。所以我的第四件工作是送藥。

　　送藥正送得起勁，一個傢伙來找我，他說：「修士，我是開救護車的，你要幫我抬四個遺體到車上去。」我曾背部受傷過，重東西早就不抬了，可是修士是什麼都要做的，我只好去抬。好在遺體都已用白布包好，我看不見他們什麼樣子。

51-55　　上車以前，我抓了一位年輕力壯的修士與我同行，因為我畢竟不是修士，也不懂當地法律，萬一有人找起我麻煩來，我應付不了。那位修士覺得有道理，就和我一起去了。這位修士十九歲左右，身強體壯，一看就可以知道出身富有家庭，否則不會體格如此之好，他在一所大學念了一年電機，就決定修道，參加這個修會。這位修士其實是個漂亮的年輕人，只是臉上有一個胎記，使他看上去好像臉上有一個刀疤，他就是昨天在彌撒中打鼓的那一位，他十分外向，老是在講笑話，途中我想買一瓶可口可樂喝，他說他不可以接受我的可口可樂，他說他不戴錶，曾經有人要送一只錶，他也沒接受。他說他唯一財產

◇ tedious（adj.）冗長的；煩累的
◇ overjoyed（adj.）大喜過望的
◇ relaxing and enjoyable 輕鬆愉快

◇ fill（v.）配藥；抓藥（註：in charge of filling the prescriptions 為「負責照處方抓藥」之意）

My third job was washing clothes, a very tedious task. As I washed, yet another person called me "Brother" and told me to take medicine to the patients. I was overjoyed, since this job was relaxing and enjoyable. A young man was in charge of filling the prescriptions; once he finished, we handed them out to the patients one by one. So my fourth job was handing out medicine.

As I was enthusiastically delivering medicine, a fellow came looking for me. "Brother, I'm the ambulance driver," said he. "I need you to help me lift four bodies into the cab." I had injured my back once before, so I hadn't lifted heavy things for a long time, but a monk has to do everything, so I couldn't refuse. Fortunately, the bodies had already been wrapped in white cloth, so I couldn't see what they looked like.

51-55

CD2-9

Before getting into the ambulance, I grabbed a young, strong monk to come with me because, after all, I was no monk, and I didn't understand the local laws— if someone were to make trouble for me, I wouldn't know what to do. He saw my point and agreed to come along. This monk was about nineteen and strongly built. A glance was enough to see that he came from a rich family— otherwise he wouldn't have been in such fine shape. He had studied electrical engineering at a university for a year before deciding to become a monk of Mother Teresa's order. He was actually quite a handsome

◇ injure (v.) 傷害；損傷
◇ point (n.) 用意；意思 (註：saw my point 為「看出我的意思」、「瞭解我的用意」之意)

◇ (in) shape (n.) (尤其指身體狀況方面) 健康

是三套衣服、一雙鞋，萬一鞋子壞了，可能要等一陣子才會有新的給他，他滿不在乎地說，我可以赤腳走路。說到赤腳，他拍一下他的大腿，痛痛快快地說：「我要一輩子做一個窮人，做到我死為止。」他說的時候，滿臉笑容，快樂得很。

我在想這小子，如果不做修士，一定有一大批女生追他，他一定可以過好日子，可是他現在什麼都沒有了，只有三套衣服，可是他那種嘻嘻哈哈的樣子，好像他已擁有了一切。

火葬場到了，這所火葬場有一大片房子，房子裡外全是乞丐。我們三人將遺體搬到一個炭堆上，就放在哪裡，什麼時候火葬，我們不知道。我感到這好像在丟垃圾，使我非常難過，有一個遺體的布後來散了，我認出這是一個年輕人的遺體，他昨天什麼都不吃，一位修士情急之下，找了極像奧黛利赫本的義工來餵他，卻也動不了他求死的決

◇ birthmark 胎記
◇ outgoing (adj.) 外向的；開朗的
◇ undaunted (adj.) 無畏的

◇ barefoot (adv.) 赤著腳地；沒穿鞋地（註：walk barefoot 為「打赤腳走路」之意）
◇ radiate (v.) 散放；發出

young man, but he had a birthmark on his face that looked like a scar. He was the one who had played drums at Mass the day before. He was very outgoing, always telling jokes. On the way, I wanted to buy him a Coke, but he said he couldn't accept it. He said he didn't wear a watch— someone had once wanted to give him one, but he didn't accept it either. He said his only possessions were three sets of clothes and a pair of shoes. If the shoes wore out, he might have to wait a while before getting new ones. Completely undaunted by that prospect, he said he could walk barefoot. As he mentioned being barefoot, he slapped his leg and said with great pleasure, "I want to be a poor man all my life, until the day I die." As he spoke, his smiling face radiated happiness.

I thought, if this lad hadn't become a monk, there would surely be a whole pack of girls chasing after him. He could have lived comfortably, but now he had nothing— just three sets of clothes. Yet his happy, carefree manner made it seem as though he had everything.

We arrived at the crematory, where there was a big building filled with beggars. The three of us lifted the bodies onto a pile of charcoal and left them there, not knowing when they would be cremated. It seemed like we were throwing away garbage, I thought, and felt sick at heart. The cloth covering one of the bodies slipped aside, and I recognized that it was the body of a young man who hadn't eaten anything the day before. A monk, desperate to help, found a volunteer

---

◇ chase (v.) 追求；追趕
◇ carefree (adj.) 無憂無慮的
◇ crematory (n.) 火葬場

◇ slip (v.) 滑；溜 (註：slipped aside 為「滑掉」、「滑到一旁」之意)
◇ desperate (adj.) 急切的

心，昨天下午就去世了。還好死前有人握了他的手，據說他在垂死之家四進四出，好了就出去流浪，得了病又回來，最後一次，他已喪失鬥志，不吃飯不喝水，也幾乎不肯吃藥，只求人家握住他的手。

遺體放好，我們一轉身，兩隻大烏鴉立刻飛下來啄食，牠們先用腳熟練地扯開白布，然後就一口一口地吃起來。死者的手，原來放在身上的，因為布被拉開，我眼看他的右手慢慢地垂了下來，碰到了地。布一旦被拉開，我也看到了他的臉，兩隻眼睛沒有閉，對著天上望著，滿臉淒苦的表情。我們都嚇壞了，跑回去趕烏鴉，我找到了一塊大木板，將遺體蓋上，可是頭和腳仍露在外面。

雖然只有幾秒鐘的時間，那位孩子無語問蒼天的淒苦表情，以及大烏鴉來啄食的情景，已使我受不了了。

56-60　　回來以後，還有一件事在等著我，又有人叫我：「修士，我要你幫忙，」原來我們要抬垃圾去倒，垃圾中包含了死者的衣物。垃圾場要

◇ practically（adv.）幾乎；差不多　　　◇ peck（v.）啄

who looked just like Audrey Hepburn to feed him, but even that could not shake his determination to die. He passed away that afternoon. At least someone held his hand before he died. I heard that he had been in and out of the Home for the Dying many times: each time he got better, he went out to wander; when he got sick again he came back. In the end, he lost the will to keep fighting. He didn't eat, didn't drink and practically refused to take medicine. All he asked was that someone hold his hand.

After we had laid out the bodies, as soon as we turned to leave, two big crows immediately flew down and started pecking. First they pulled away the cloth with practiced claws, and then they began eating, one mouthful at a time. One dead boy's arms had been resting on his body, but after the cloth was pulled away, I saw his right arm slowly droop down to the ground. When the cloth was pulled away, I also saw his face: with unclosed eyes, he stared toward the sky with a face full of anguish. Shocked, we ran back and drove away the crows, and I found a big board with which to cover the bodies. But their heads and feet were still left exposed.

Though it only lasted for a few seconds, the look of hopeless, resigned anguish on the child's face, along with the sight of the crows pecking his body, was more than I could stand.

When I got back, there was something else waiting for me. Once again someone called to me, "Brother, I need your help." Our task

56-60

◇ practiced（adj.）熟練的
◇ anguish（n.）痛苦

◇ exposed（adj.）外露的
◇ stand（n.）忍耐；承受

走五分鐘，還沒有走到，一堆小孩子就來搶，垃圾堆上起碼有三十隻大烏鴉在爭食，更有一大批男女老少在垃圾堆裡找東西。

貧窮，貧窮，貧窮，這次我真的看到了貧窮所帶來的悲慘，由於大家的推推拉拉，我的衣服完全遭了殃，我當時還穿了圍裙，圍裙一下子就變髒了。

我的心頭沉重無比，這種景象，以前，我只在電視和報紙上看到，現在，活生生地呈現在我的面前。

回到垂死之家，一位修女下令叫我去教堂祈禱，他說修士們都已去了，我也該去。修士們果真在，那位陪我去的修士盤腿而坐，兩手分開，低頭默想，看上去像在坐禪，嘻皮笑臉的表情完全沒有了。

而我呢？我坐在他們後面，還沒有坐穩，我的眼淚就泉湧而出，我終於瞭解了德蕾莎修女的話：

◇ garbage dump（n.）垃圾場

◇ contents（n.）（包裝或容器裡所盛裝的）東西或內容物（注意：作這方面意思解釋時恆為複數形式）

◇ trash pile 垃圾堆

◇ refuse [`rɛfjus]（n.）垃圾；利用過後不要的東西

was to take out the trash, which included clothing that had belonged to the dead. The garbage dump was a five-minute walk away, but before we arrived, a flock of children came to fight over the contents of the trash. On top of the trash pile, there were at least thirty crows competing for food, while a mob of people, male and female, young and old, picked through the refuse.

Poverty, poverty, poverty— this time I really saw the misery which poverty brings. With everyone pushing and pulling around me, my clothes were ruined, and the apron I was wearing at the time became filthy in a moment.

My heart felt unbearably heavy within me. In the past, I had only seen scenes like this on TV or in the newspaper, but now I was right in the middle of one.

After I returned to the Home for the Dying, a nun ordered me to the chapel to pray. She said all the monks were already there, so I should go too. Sure enough, the monks were there. The one who had gone with me to the crematory was sitting Indian style, his hands apart, his head down, pondering silently, as though he were meditating. His joyful, carefree manner of before was completely gone.

And me? I sat down behind them, but before I had even sat all the way down, tears began to flow freely. I finally understood Mother Teresa's words:

◇ misery (n.) 痛苦；悲慘
◇ ruin (v.) 摧毀；破壞
◇ filthy (adj.) 骯髒的；污穢的
◇ unbearably (adv.) 無法忍受地

一顆純潔的心，

會自由地給，

自由地愛，

直到它受到創傷。

61-65 我過去也號稱為窮人服務過，可是我總找些愉快的事做，我在監獄裡服務時，老是找一些受過教育的年輕人做朋友，絕不敢安慰死刑犯，不僅怕看到手銬和腳鐐，更怕陪他們走向死亡，我不敢面對人類最悲慘的事。

現在我仍在做義工，可是是替一群在孤兒院的孩子們服務，這群孩子，被修女們慣壞了，個個活潑可愛而且快樂，替他們服務不僅不會心痛，反而會有歡樂。

我雖然也替窮人服務過，可總不敢替「最窮」的人服務，我一直有意無意地躲避人類的真正窮困和不幸。因此，我雖然給過，也愛過，可是我始終沒有「心靈受到創傷」的經驗，現在我才知道，其實我從來沒有真正地愛、真正地給過。

◇ claim(v.)宣稱（註：在這裡引申為「大言不慚地說」）

◇ educated(adj.)受過教育的

◇ death row 死刑

◇ handcuffs and shackles 手銬腳鐐

◇ prospect(n.)前景

A pure heart
Will give freely
And love freely
Until it is wounded

In the past, I had claimed to have served the poor, but in reality I had always found things to do that made me happy. When I served in prisons, I would always seek out a few educated young people to make friends with— I utterly lacked the courage to comfort the prisoners on death row. It was not merely that I feared to see their handcuffs and shackles— it was that I was afraid to stand beside them as they faced the prospect of death. I lacked the courage to face the greatest of human misery.

61-65

I still volunteer, but now I serve a group of children at an orphanage. Those kids have been spoiled rotten by the nuns there— each one of them is beautiful, happy and full of life. Serving them is not only painless but even uplifting.

Although I have served the poor, I've never had the courage to serve the "poorest of the poor." Whether consciously or not, I've always avoided the real poverty and misfortune of humankind. Hence, though I have given, and though I have loved, I have never experienced "wounds of the heart." Now, at last, I understand: I have never really loved before, nor have I ever really given.

◇ spoil（v.）寵愛（註：have been spoiled rotten 為「已經被寵壞了」）
◇ uplifting（adj.）令人振奮的；使人心情好的
◇ consciously（adv.）有意識地；有知覺地
◇ experience（v.）經歷；遭遇

可是五十六年來舒適的日子，忽然被這兩小時的悲慘情景所取代，想起那四位死者，其中一位低垂的手，對著蒼天望的雙眼。此時窗外正好下著大雨，他不僅在露天中被雨淋，還要被烏鴉啄，我這次確確實實地感到難過到極點了。

耶穌的苦像在我前面，我又看到了「我渴」，做了四十年的基督徒，今天才明瞭了當年耶穌所說「我渴」的意義，可是我敢自稱是基督徒嗎？當基督說「我渴」的時候，我大概在研究室裡做研究，或在咖啡館裡喝咖啡。

66-70　我向來不太會祈禱，可是這一次我感到我在和耶穌傾談，我痛痛快快地和耶穌聊天，也痛痛快快地流淚，淚流了一陣子，反而感到一種心靈上的平安。我感謝天主給我這個抬死人遺體和到垃圾場的機會。我感到我似乎沒有白活這輩子。抬起頭來，卻發現那位修士坐在我的旁邊，他顯然看到我流淚，來安慰我的。

他說：「先生，你的汗味好臭，我們都吃不消你的臭味，你看，修

◇ replace (v.) 替代；取……而代之　　　◇ soak (v.) 溼潤；溼透
◇ witness (v.) 目擊；親眼看見　　　◇ unspeakable (adj.) 說不出的

But all of a sudden, fifty-six years of comfortable living had gone out the window, replaced by two hours of witnessing real misery. I thought of the four dead bodies, including the one with the drooping arm and the eyes staring heavenward. At the time, it happened to be raining hard outside— not only was he being soaked out in the open, but he was being pecked at by crows. An unspeakable pain tore at my heart.

A crucifix hung in front of me: once again I saw the words, "I thirst." After forty years of being a Christian, I finally understood what Jesus meant when He said those words. But did I dare call myself a Christian? When Christ said, "I thirst," I was probably in the lab doing research, or maybe in a café drinking coffee.

I've never been much good at praying, but this time I felt I was really speaking to Jesus. As my tears flowed freely, I poured out my soul to Him. After I had cried for a good while, I actually felt an inner peace. I thanked the Lord for giving me the opportunity to carry those corpses and visit that garbage dump. I felt as though my life had not been in vain. As I lifted my head, I was surprised to see my friend the monk standing by my side. He must have seen me weeping and come to comfort me.

66-70

He said, "Sir, your sweat stinks. None of us can stand your foul odor. Look, your smell has driven all the monks away, and now I'm

---

◇ research（n.）研究（註：doing research 為「做研究」）
◇ corpse（n.）屍體

◇ weep（v.）哭泣
◇ stink（v.）發臭
◇ foul odor 惡臭

士們都被你臭走了，現在只有我肯陪你，你比印度人臭得多了。」

　　我知道他是來安慰我的，雖然我汗流浹背，衣服全濕了，也的確臭得厲害，可是他笑我比印度人臭，總不能默認，因此我做了一手勢假裝要打他一拳。

　　當時我們仍在聖堂內，這種胡鬧實在有點不像話。我們同時走到聖堂外面去，那位修士，四處張望一下，發現無人在場，做了一個中國功夫的姿勢，意思是如果我要揍他，他武功更好。

　　他說其他義工都只穿短褲和 T 恤，只有我穿了一件襯衫和長褲，修士們都穿襯衫和長褲，我當時又沒有帶手錶，才會被人誤認為修士。他調皮地說，「下次再來，一定仍由你去火葬場，你最像抬遺體的人。」我聽了以後，心裡舒服多了。

71-75　　離開垂死之家以前，我又幫忙洗了碗。

◇ accusation（n.）指控
◇ swing（v.）揮（拳）
◇ inappropriate（adj.）不妥的；不當的

◇ pose（n.）姿勢；架勢（註：did a Chinese kung fu pose 意為「擺出一個中國功夫架勢」）

the only one left who's willing to stay with you. You smell worse than an Indian!"

I knew he had come to comfort me. Although my back was covered in sweat, my clothes were soaked with it and I certainly smelled bad enough, his accusation that I smelled worse than an Indian was more than I was willing to take quietly. So I swung my arm around, pretending I was about to punch him.

As we were still in the chapel at the time, we both felt it was a little inappropriate to play around like that, so we walked outside. The monk, looking around to make sure no one was watching, did a Chinese kung fu pose, meaning that if I was thinking of beating him up, his kung fu was stronger.

He said the other volunteers only wore shorts and T-shirts; I was the only one wearing a dress shirt and long pants, which is what all the monks wear. Also, I wasn't wearing a watch, so that was why people kept mistaking me for a monk. He said mischievously, "Next time you come, you'll definitely get sent to the crematory again. You look just like a corpse-bearer." After hearing that, I felt much better.

Before I left the Home for the Dying, I washed the dishes again. 　71-75

◇ shorts (n.)（恆為複數）短褲　　◇ mischievously (adv.)惡作劇地；淘氣地；調皮地

　　在大門口，這位修士背了一只麻布口袋準備離去，口袋上寫著：M.C.，他看到了我，對我說：「明天我不來這裡，」然後他調皮地說「修士，再見。」

　　我注視他的麻布口袋，以及他衣服上的十字架。好羨慕他，他看出我的心情，兩手合一地說：「只要你繼續流汗，流到身體發臭，你就和我們在一起。」

　　我也兩手合一地說：「天主保佑你，我們下次見面，恐怕是在天堂了。」我看到他拿起袖子來，偷偷地擦眼淚。

　　第二天，我坐計程車去機場，又看到了一位修士和一位日本義工在照顧一位躺在街上的垂死老人，今天清晨，老人的家人將他抬來，遺棄在街頭。修士在叫計程車，日本義工跪下來握住老人的手。他是醫學院的學生，看到我，他說，「絕無希望。」雖然也許真的沒有希望，可是這位老人至少知道，世上仍有人關懷他的。

76-80　　我當時恨不得不再走回計程車，留下來永遠地服務。

◇ teasingly (adv.) 戲謔地；作弄地　　　◇ sweat (v.) 流汗

At the front door, the monk had a gunny sack on his back as he prepared to leave. On the bag were written the letters "M. C." (Missionaries of Charity). When he saw me, he said, "I won't be here tomorrow." Then he added teasingly, "Goodbye, monk."

I gazed at his gunny sack and the cross on his clothes; I envied him. He saw what I was thinking, and with his hands clasped together he said, "As long as you keep sweating until you stink, you'll always be one of us."

With my hands clasped together likewise, I replied, "God bless you. I'm afraid the next time we meet will be in Heaven." I saw him pull up his sleeve and furtively wipe a tear away.

As I rode a taxi to the airport the next day, I saw a monk and a Japanese volunteer taking care of a dying old man in the street. Earlier in the morning, the old man's family had brought him there to abandon him. The monk was calling for a cab, and the Japanese volunteer was kneeling down holding the old man's hand. He was a medical student; when he saw me, he said, "No hope at all." Although perhaps there really was no hope for him to live, at least the old man now knew that there were still people in the world who cared about him.

At that moment, I genuinely wished that I could stay and serve there forever instead of having to walk back to the taxi.

◇ furtively(adv.)暗中地；偷偷摸摸地　　◇ genuinely(adv.)真誠地；真心地
◇ kneel(v.)跪

雖然只有兩天，垂死之家的經驗使我永生難忘。

我忘不了加爾各答街上無家可歸的人。

我忘不了一個小男孩用杯子在陰溝裡盛水喝。

我忘不了兩個小孩每晚都睡在我住的旅館門口，只有他們兩人，最大的頂多四歲。

81-85　　我忘不了垂死之家裡面骨瘦如柴的病人。

我忘不了那位年輕的病人，一有機會就希望我能握住他的手。

我忘不了人的遺體被放在一堆露天的煤渣上，野狗和烏鴉隨時會來吃他們，暴風雨也會隨時來淋濕他們。他們的眼睛望著天。

我忘不了垃圾場附近衣不蔽體的窮人，他們和野狗和烏鴉沒有什麼不同，沒有人類應有的任何一絲尊嚴。

◇ drench (v.) 使溼透

Although it only lasted for two days, I will never forget my experience at the Home for the Dying.

I'll never forget the homeless people on the streets of Calcutta.

I'll never forget the boy drinking the gutter water he had scooped up with his cup.

I'll never forget the two children who slept at the entrance to my hotel every night. There were only two of them, and the older one couldn't have been more than four.

I'll never forget the pencil-thin patients at the Home for the Dying. ⁸¹⁻⁸⁵

I'll never forget the sick youth who asked me to hold his hand as soon as he got the chance.

I'll never forget placing those corpses on a pile of charcoal with no roof overhead, where at any moment, wild dogs and crows might come, or a rainstorm might drench them. Their eyes were staring heavenward.

I'll never forget the poor souls at the trash dump, clothed in rags that hardly covered their bodies. No different from dogs or crows, they had not a scrap of human dignity to call their own.

◇ scrap (n.)丁點；小片(註：had not a scrap of human dignity 為「連一丁點做人的尊嚴都沒有」)

可是我也忘不了德蕾莎修女兩手合一的祝福，和她慈祥的微笑。

86-90　我更忘不了修士修女們無限的愛心和耐心。

我忘不了修士修女們過著貧窮生活時心安理得的神情。

我忘不了那麼多的義工，什麼工作都肯做。

我忘不了那位日本義工單腿跪下握住乞丐手的姿態。

雖然我看見人類悲慘的一面，我也從來沒有見過如此多善良的人。德蕾莎修女最大的貢獻，是她將關懷和愛帶到人類最黑暗的角落，我們更應該感謝的是她感動多少人，多少人因此變得更加善良，我應該就是其中的一個。

讓高牆倒下吧

91-95　德蕾莎修女當年並不一定要走出高牆的。

◇ infinite [ˋɪnfənɪt] (adj.) 無限的；無盡的

But likewise, I'll never forget the blessings Mother Teresa gave with her hands clasped together, nor will I forget her kind smile.

I'll also never forget the infinite love and patience of her monks and nuns.　86-90

I'll never forget the peace and tranquility the monks and nuns found in their lives of poverty.

I'll never forget all those volunteers, who would do any job they were given.

I'll never forget the way the Japanese volunteer knelt down on one knee and held that beggar's hand.

Although I had witnessed human misery in its rawest form, yet never had I seen people so full of goodness. Mother Teresa's greatest contribution is bringing care and love into the darkest corner of humanity, but we should be just as grateful to her for touching so many hearts, for making so many people better than they were before. And one of those people, no doubt, is me.

Let the Wall Fall

Mother Teresa did not have to step outside of the wall that day.　91-95

◇ contribution (n.) 貢獻

　　她可以成立一個基金會，雇用一些職員，利用電腦和媒體，替窮人募款，然後找人將錢「施捨」給窮人。

　　她也可以只是白天去看看窮人，晚上仍回來過歐洲式舒適的生活。

　　甚至她只要每週有一天去服務窮人一下，其他的日子都替富人服務。

　　可是她自己變成了窮人，因為她要親手握住貧窮人的手，伴他們步向死亡，再也不會逃避世上有窮人的殘酷事實。她不僅照顧印度的窮人，也照顧愛滋病患，最近，高棉很多人被地雷炸成了殘廢，沒有輪椅可坐，德蕾莎修女已親自去面對這個事實。

96-100　　她單槍匹馬走入貧民窟，勇敢地將世人的悲慘背在自己身上。

　　她完全走出了高牆。

　　我們每個人都在心裡築了一道高牆，我們要在高牆內過著天堂般的

◇ media (n.) 媒體
◇ dole (out) (v.) 施捨；分配

◇ maim (v.) 使 (某人) 殘廢；使 (某人) 肢體成殘

She could have established a foundation, hired some workers, and used technology and the media to raise funds for the poor, then gotten people to dole it out to them.

She could also have just gone out to see the poor during the daytime, returning to her comfortable European lifestyle at night.

She could even have served the poor briefly one day every week, then spent the rest of her time serving the rich.

But she herself became poor, for she wanted to hold their hands with her hands, to be by their side as they faced death, to never again attempt to escape the cold, hard fact that there are needy people in the world. She cares not only for the poor of India, but for AIDS patients as well. Recently in Cambodia, many people have been maimed by land mines, and they have no wheelchairs to sit in. Mother Teresa has already faced this fact.

Alone, with no one by her side to assist her, she walks into ghettoes 96-100 and courageously takes upon herself the misery of the world.

She has stepped completely outside of the wall.

All of us have built a wall around our hearts. We want to live our own heavenly lives within that wall while pushing hell outside of it. That way, we can blissfully pretend that there is no misery among

◇ land mine 地雷　　　　　　◇ ghetto [ˋgɛto] (n.) 貧民窟

生活，而將地獄推到高牆之外。這樣，我們可以心安理得假裝人間沒有悲慘。儘管有人餓死，我們仍可以大吃大喝。

讓高牆倒下吧，只要高牆倒下，我們就可以有一顆寬廣的心。

有了寬廣的心，我們會看見世上不幸的人，也會聽到他們的哀求「我渴」。

101-104 看見了人類的不幸，我們會有熾熱的愛。

有了熾熱的愛，我們會開始替不幸的人服務。

替不幸的人服務，一定會帶來我們心靈上的創傷，可是心靈上的創傷一定會最後帶來心靈上的平安。

如果你是基督徒，容我再加一句話，只有經過這個過程，我們才能進入永生。

◇ fill（n.）飽足；滿足　　　　◇ broaden（v.）拓寬；使……開濶

humankind. Even though there are people dying of hunger, we can go on eating and drinking our fill.

Let the wall fall. If we would just let the wall fall, our hearts would broaden and deepen.

With broader, deeper hearts, we would see the world's unfortunate and hear them crying, "I thirst."

With a clear view of human misfortune, we would be filled with a consuming love.　101-104

With that consuming love, we would start serving the less fortunate.

Serving the less fortunate will bring wounds of sorrow to our hearts.
But wounds of the heart always bring peace in the end.

If you're a Christian, permit me to add one final word:
This is the only way by which we can enter into eternal life.

◇ consuming (adj.) 強烈的　　　◇ eternal life 永生

(1) on the whole 大致上；一般說來(1段)

On the whole they lived lives of comfort and ease
一般說來，她們的生活是相當安定而且舒適的。

解析

這個片語一般放在句首或者句中的位置，whole 是「整體」、「完整」的意思，從字面上不難看出整個片語的意思來。即使在中文裡，這也是個使用度很高的用語。此外，讀者可以看到「舒適安逸的生活」的英文為 a life(lives)of comfort and ease；所以 live a life(lives)of comfort and ease 就是「過著舒適安逸的生活」。

小試身手

1. 他的表現整體上來說在水準之上。

_____

(2) have a huge adverse impact on... 對⋯⋯造成極大不利(不良)的影響(3段)

World War II broke out, and the transport of soldiers had a huge adverse impact on the transport of food.
二次世界大戰爆發，糧食運輸因為軍隊的運輸而受了極大的影響。

解析

impact 作「衝擊」、「影響」解釋，adverse 為「不利的」、「有害的」，整個片語綜合起來的意思也就很清楚了。或許你想問：如果要表示「對⋯⋯造成有利的影響」該怎麼表示，那你只要想辦法把 adverse 改為 favorable 就好了。

小試身手

2. 專家說森林火災有時候對山區生態造成有利的影響(有利於山區生
　　態)。

_____

(3) What little... 僅有少量的……；僅有微薄的……(3段)

Multitudes of farmers had had but little savings to begin with, and now
what little they did have vanished with inflation.

大批農人本來就沒有多少儲蓄，現在這些儲蓄因為通貨膨脹而化為烏
有。

解析

這個句型比較特殊，多數的讀者可能會覺得奇怪怎麼用了 what little 這兩
個字？其實，原來的句子應該是 ...and now the little(savings)that they did
have vanished with inflation. 程度不錯的讀者很快就可以領悟過來，what
little... 原來就是 the little that... 的綜合。

小試身手

3. 他在背後說朋友的壞話而失去了僅有少數的朋友。

_____

(4) in the eyes of... 在(某人)眼裡；在(某人)看來(6段)

But in the eyes of these European nuns, India was a backward country—such scenes of misery were nothing out of the ordinary.

可是對這些來自歐洲的修女們，印度是一個落後的國家，這種悲慘情景不算什麼特別。

解析

片語本身的意思夠清楚，讀者不妨趁機會學習同句子中，幾個重要的字詞用法，「落後國家」為 a backward country；nothing out of the ordinary 的意思為「不算什麼特別」、「沒什麼了不得」。請注意 out of the ordinary 為「不尋常」、「很特殊」的意思。

小試身手

4. 在他父母親眼裡，他比莫札特更有音樂才華。

_____

(5) (be) similar to... 和……相似；近似於……(9段)

She took off her thick, heavy, European-style black habit and exchanged it for a light white garment with blue trim, similar to what Indian farm women wear.

她脫下了那套厚重的黑色歐洲式修女道袍，換上了一件像印度農婦穿的白色衣服，這套衣服有藍色的邊。

解析

similar 本身為「相似的」之意，是個形容詞，所以經常放在 be 動詞之後，而讀者要特別注意後面所接的介詞 to 本身即帶有「鄰近」、「接近」的意思。dissimilar 為 similar 的反義字，意思和 different 接近，所以後面所接的介詞為 from 以表示「區別」、「差異」的意思。

> **小試身手**
>
> 5. 兩國在文化淵源彼此相似。
>
> _____

（6）keep one's chin up 昂然不屈；不氣餒（10段）

This was eccentric even in the eyes of the Catholic church— a lot of priests thought she was gravely misguided— but her faith continually supported her, enabling her to keep her chin up no matter how hard things got.

這仍是怪事，很多神父認為她大錯特錯，可是她的信仰一直支持著她，使她在遭遇多少挫折之後仍不氣餒。

解析

歷經滄桑，受盡折磨，還能不屈不撓昂首挺立的人，常是我們欽佩崇拜的對象。怎麼「昂首」挺立、「昂然」不屈呢？當然是要把下巴 chin 伸出伸直，而這個動作就是 keep one's chin up 囉。

> **小試身手**
>
> 6. 他所有的同伴都放棄退出，但是他不屈不撓，奮力向前。
>
> _____

(7) become a household name 成了家喻戶曉的人物(11段)

Now, forty-six years later, Mother Teresa has become a household name.
到今天,四十六年以後,德蕾莎修女已是家喻戶曉的人物。

解析

某人知名度很高,聲名遠播,大多數人也許沒見過他本人,但是提到他的豐功偉業,一般人也都能夠說得出幾樣,隨便一打聽,多數人也都知道有這號人物,中文說「家喻戶曉的人物」,而英文就以 a household name 表達之。且可同時形容知名公司或機構。

小試身手

7. 也許你不知道Costco是什麼,但是在美國它可是赫赫有名、家喻戶曉。

_____

(8) There is nothing(remotely)resembling... 連個…… 都沒有 (13段)

There is nothing remotely resembling a computer.
電腦等一概沒有。

解析

譯者在這裡把「一概沒有」處理的非常絕妙,真是神來之筆。就字面看,這個句型的意思為「沒有酷似……的東西」,remotely 這個字用得極妙,它的本意為傳達出「偏遠的」,但是在這裡它和 resembling 合作,共同營造出「一點相似之處都沒有」的意思來。在中文裡我們常說「連個像樣的東西都沒有」也就是這樣子的意思了。

8. 沒有地方可以讓你膜拜。那個小村落連個像樣的小教堂都沒有。

_____

（9）the poorest of the poor 窮到不能再窮的人（15段）

The nuns and monks take an oath to spend the rest of their lives in sincere, devoted service to the poorest of the poor.

修士修女們宣誓終其一生要全心全意地為「最窮」的人服務。

解析

放鬆心情，欣賞一下修辭吧。最近中文流行「……到不行」，某某人天資駑鈍，我們就說他「笨到不行」，某某人數學特厲害，什麼題目都難不倒他，真是高手中的高手，「厲害到不行」。遇到這樣的狀況，用類似這種句型可以傳達得很貼切。

9. 同學們都找他請教數學問題。他們認為他是高手中的高手。

_____

(10) be coldly indifferent to somebody 不加理睬（某人）；冷漠以對（某人）(21段)

When a poor man is homeless, he doesn't just wish for a place to stay, but that no one will ever abandon him, forget him, or be coldly indifferent to him again.

窮人無家可歸，不僅希望有一間小屋可以棲身，而且也希望再也沒有人遺棄他，忘了他，對他漠不關心。

解析

indifferent 是形容詞，本身即是「冷淡」、「不關心」的意思，前面常放 be 動詞，而後面的介詞常接 to，表示「對……冷漠」。

小試身手

10. 他只關心一己的利益（除了他自己的利益他對什麼都冷漠不關心）。

_____

(11) be devoid of... 缺少……；沒有……(23段)

She knows there are too many people in the world whose lives are so devoid of dignity that they are barely human lives at all, and she must take care of them first.

她知道世界上太多人過著毫無尊嚴的非人生活，她必須先照顧他們。

解析

devoid 是形容詞，是「缺乏」、「沒有」的意思，介詞 of 常尾隨其後。整個片語表示「空無一物」、「什麼都沒有」的意思。

小試身手

11. 外太空是個除了極度寒冷、漆黑與寂靜之外，什麼都沒有的地方。

＿＿＿＿＿＿＿＿＿＿＿＿＿＿＿＿＿＿＿＿＿＿＿＿＿＿＿＿

（12）**come to a true understanding of...** 瞭解⋯⋯的真義；真正
　　 搞懂⋯⋯（27段）

I finally came to a true understanding of the relationship between
"wounds of the heart" and love.
我才真正了解所謂「心靈受傷」和愛的關係。

解析

大多數人看到「真正了解」時心裡想到的英文不外乎是 truly understand，其
實把動詞 understand 改成動名詞 understanding，把副詞 truly 改為形容詞
true，然後消失掉的動詞（即 understand）用 come to 取代之，所傳達的依
然是同樣的意思。

小試身手

12. 幾番錯誤的嘗試後，我終於約略知道那是怎麼回事。

＿＿＿＿＿＿＿＿＿＿＿＿＿＿＿＿＿＿＿＿＿＿＿＿＿＿＿＿

(13) haggle back and forth about... 討價還價；一來一往磋商 (31段)

Then we haggled back and forth about how long she could stay in Taiwan. Eventually she agreed to stay for four days.

然後我們又討價還價地講她究竟能在台灣待幾天，她最後同意四天。

解析

haggle 原本的意思是拿著刀斧大力揮砍的動作，back 是向後，forth 是向前，整個片語所傳達出來「殺價」、「砍價錢」的意思非常的明顯。

小試身手

13. 她覺得賺到了。她討價還價快半小時。

_____

(14) drag on 拖延(33段)

Things dragged on for several minutes, and as there were still twenty people behind me, I was forced to cut our meeting short.

折騰了幾分鐘，後面還有二十幾個人，我只好結束了會面。

解析

動詞 drag 本身即是「牽引」、「拖拉」而介副詞 on(請注意是介副詞而不是介詞，也就是原本為介詞 on 在這裡是副詞的作用)則帶有「繼續」、「向前」的意思，因而整個片語就表達了「繼續往前拖拉」的意思，和初學英文的人所碰到的 go on 差不多意思和用法。本句還有個很不錯的片語 cut short；動詞 cut 是「切、割、裁、剪」而 short 是「短」，兩者合起來使用，自然傳達出「縮短」的意思來。

14. 貴賓介紹沒完沒了，聽眾裡有些人開始打哈欠發牢騷。

_____

(15) a thought occurs (occurred) to somebody 某人忽然心生一念 (35段)

It was then that a thought occurred to her: if someone had talked with him as he was about to leave this world, he would no doubt have passed away more peacefully.

當時她有一個想法，如果有人在他臨走以前和他談談，一定可以使他比較平安地死去。

解析

中國學生尤其要注意這種很特別的表達法。中文習慣說某人忽然心生一念，以「人」為主詞而以「心生一念」為動詞。但英文則反其道而行，以「心念 (a thought)」為主詞，以「發生；產生 (occur to)」為動詞，而以「人」為受詞，要注意因為 occur 是不及物動詞，所以在後面接受詞之前要先加上介詞 to。另外有件很重要的事情要注意，因為動詞 occur 的重音節在最後一個音節 (-cur)，而且最後的音節是一個母音字母 (u) 和一個子音字母 (r)，所以在加上 -ed 或者 -ing 之前都要重複這最後一個字音字母 (r) 而變成 occurred 和 occurring 的形式。

15. 我忽然想到一個很好的點子而迫不及待說給我的好友們聽。

_____

（16）for fear of... 因恐……；唯恐……（38段）

The streets of Calcutta are filled with the homeless: one has to tread carefully at night for fear of bumping into someone sleeping on the ground.

加爾各答滿街都是無家可歸的人，晚上出去必須小心走路，不然一定會碰到睡在地上的人。

解析

介詞 for 表「因為」，名詞 fear 則為「恐懼」、「害怕」之意，合起來就是「因恐」、「唯恐」的意思。

小試身手

16. 我再三檢查門窗，唯恐有人闖入。

_____

（17）be（totally）absorbed in... 專注於……；完全投入於……（43段）

Like African-Americans singing spirituals, these monks were totally absorbed in their music.

這些男修士唱歌的時候，活像美國黑人唱靈歌一樣地陶醉。

解析

動詞 absorb 本意為「吸收」，用在這種「被動」的結構（be absorbed）卻演變出「專注；完全投入」的意思。表達某人做什麼事情心無旁鶩，好似整個人被所做的事情吸進去了，難以自拔。

小試身手

17. 他很專注看雜誌，連我進來他都沒注意到。

_____

(18) hail from... 來自……(45段)

The vast majority were from Europe, while others hailed from Japan and Singapore.

絕大多數的義工來自歐洲，也有來自日本和新加坡的。

解析

hail 作動詞時，是「歡呼」、「招呼致意」或「下冰雹」；名詞時則為「冰雹」的意思。冰雹從天而降，所以 hail from 就和 come from 一樣，表示某人「從何處而來」「是何方人士」的意思。此外，你注意到了嗎？中文「絕大多數」的英文相等語為 the vast majority。

小試身手

18. 來自姊妹市的朋友們每人獲贈一袋紀念品。

_____

(19)（habits）are hard to break （習慣）改不掉；無法革除（習慣）（48段）

... and though he was now abandoned, his old habits were hard to break.
……現在被人家遺棄，積習仍未改。

解析

相信大多數人知道「養成（好／壞）習慣」所使用的動詞為 form 或 develop 或 cultivate，那麼革除、改掉（壞）習慣要怎麼表達呢？英文習慣上使用 kick 或 break 或 get rid of。學過 Old habits die hard. 這個諺語嗎？它相當於中文「積習難改」這個成語，你也可以把它說成 Old habits are hard to break.。

小試身手

19. 我知道不守時是壞習慣。我會盡力把它改掉。

_____

(20)（be）in charge of Ving... 負責做……（49段）

A young man was in charge of filling the prescriptions; once he finished, we handed them out to the patients one by one.
有一位青年的修士負責配藥，配完之後，我們給一位一位病人送去。

解析

charge 在這裡是「責任」，而 in charge of 則變成是「承擔……的責任」。還有一個重點要注意，原譯文裡有個 prescription(s) 為「藥方」、「處方」的意思，而「依處方配藥」就叫作 fill the prescription，使用 fill 來當動詞。

小試身手

20. 班長應該負責有效推動班務。

_____

(21) A glance(look)was enough to see... 一望即知(51段)

A glance was enough to see that he came from a rich family— otherwise he wouldn't have been in such fine shape.

一看就可以知道他出身富有家庭，否則不會體格如此之好。

解析

glance 是「看一眼」、「張望一眼」的意思，和平常大家熟悉的 look 意思相去不遠，而句型裡的具有「知道」的意味。

小試身手

21. 和他短暫面試就足以知道他是那個職位的最佳人選。

_____

(22) feel sick at heart 痛心；難過(53段)

It seemed like we were throwing away garbage, I thought, and felt sick at heart.

我感到這好像在丟垃圾，使我非常難過。

解析

sick 是指「一種很不舒服的、很難過的感覺」，常常是指生理上的狀況，作「生病」解，當然心理上也會有難過不舒服的感覺，這時候我們就說是「傷

心」、「痛心」、「難過」。

小試身手

22. 看到他們所受的苦難沒有人不傷心難過。

_____

（23）（be）still left exposed 聽任其暴露在外（54段）

But their heads and feet were still left exposed.

可是頭和腳仍露在外面。

解析

expose 是個不太容易學的字，一般有主動的 expose oneself to 和被動的 be exposed to 兩種形態。比如我們要表達「和壞人為友，你就會受到不良影響」，英文就是 If you make friends with bad people, you expose yourself to their bad influence. 或 If you make friends with bad people, you are exposed to their bad influence. 但是在本文的句型裡，意思卻有一點小小的不同，原譯文裡的 were still left exposed 為「仍聽任其暴露在外而沒有加以遮蔽」的意思。

小試身手

23. 大部分的傢俱都搬進屋子。但是因為房子空間有限，有一小部分只好放在外面任其遭受風吹日曬。

_____

(24) right in the middle of 置身其中（58段）

In the past, I had only seen scenes like this on TV or in the newspaper, but now I was right in the middle of one.

這種景象，以前，我只在電視和報紙上看到，現在，活生生地呈現在我的面前。

解析

片語的核心字眼 middle 為「中央」、「中間」的意思，片語的前面再加上一個 right，就成了「不偏不倚，正當其中」的意思。

小試身手

24. 我們正好位處颱風的行經路線上，而被勸告搬到比較安全的地方。

_____

---

(25) be spoiled rotten 被寵壞；被慣壞（62段）

These kids have been spoiled rotten by the nuns— each one of them is beautiful, happy and full of life.

這群孩子，被修女們慣壞了，個個活潑可愛而且快樂。

解析

相對於中文「不打不成器」的英文諺語為 Spare the rod; spoil the child. 意思是說不用棍子，就會慣壞小孩子。姑且不論這個諺語有無道理，至少我們知道，spoil 有「寵壞」、「慣壞」的意思。再加上 rotten 這個字本意就是「腐敗」、「腐爛」，整個片語的意思就更加明白了。但在本文中是帶著玩笑愛憐的意味。

小試身手

25. 在老師眼中，這個被祖父母慣壞的小孩令人頭痛。

_____

---

(26) nor + 助動詞 + 主詞 + 本動詞 + ……（某人、某事、某物）也不……（63段）

Now, at last, I understand: I have never really loved before, nor have I ever really given.

現在我才知道，其實我從來沒有真正地愛、真正地給過。

解析

這個句型和文法有關，它牽涉到倒裝法。你可以看到原本應該寫為正常現在完成式的 I have ever really given 在句子裡卻寫成了 have I ever really given 的形式，助動詞 have 被放到主詞前面去了。為什麼要倒裝呢？顯然是受了否定副詞 nor 的影響，別忘了 nor 的意思為「也不」。所以我們得到結論：否定副詞置於句首會影響後面的字序採取倒裝的形式。

小試身手

26. 第一個颱風沒有侵襲本島，目前已在關島形成的那個也不會。

_____

---

(27) tear at my heart 讓（某人）痛徹心扉（64段）

An unspeakable pain tore at my heart.

我這次確確實實地感到難過到極點了。

解析

unspeakable 是「說不出來的」、「無以名狀的」之意；而動詞 tear 的意思為用很大的力道「撕扯」、「拉扯」，以這樣的力道來撕扯拉扯你的心，你能不感到痛徹心扉嗎？

小試身手

27. 她浮腫的臉和受盡虐待的故事讓我心痛不已。

_____

(28)（be）clothed in rags 衣著襤褸（84段）

I'll never forget the poor souls at the trash dump, clothed in rags that hardly covered their bodies.

我忘不了垃圾場附近衣不蔽體的窮人。

解析

如果你學過 be dressed in 這個片語，那麼只要把 dressed 改成 clothed 就得了。話說回來，clothed 用的比 dressed 來得好，因為 dressed 給人的感覺比較傾向「穿著體面光鮮」的意思。rags 本身即是「破布」、「碎布」的意思，在這個片語裡指的是身上的衣服破破爛爛，就像破碎零亂的布，披在身上，已經到了衣不蔽體的地步了。

小試身手

28. 貧民區居民衣著襤褸、房舍破爛。

_____

(29) have not... to call one's own 應有的……都沒有（84段）

No different from dogs or crows, they had not a scrap of human dignity to call their own.

他們和野狗和烏鴉沒有什麼不同，沒有人類應有的任何一絲尊嚴。

解析

譯者把這句中文英譯處理得非常好，用 a scrap of human dignity 來譯「一絲（做人的）尊嚴」，用 ... to call their own 來處理「應有的……」，從字面來看，to call one's own 的意思為「可稱之為自己的……」。

小試身手

29. 他很努力地工作，可是他連個自己的房子都沒有。

_____

(30) not only... but... as well 不僅……也……（95段）

She cares not only for the poor of India, but for AIDS patients as well.

她不僅照顧印度的窮人，也照顧愛滋病患。

解析

很多人對 not only... but also... 琅琅上口，可是並不是很多人知道，也可以將 also 改成 as well 放在句尾的位置，意思則全然相同。

小試身手

30. 他不只出錢而且還出力。

_____

小試身手解答

1. His performance is, on the whole, above average.

2. Experts say that forest fires sometimes have a favorable impact on the ecological system of the mountains.

3. He lost what few friends he had by speaking ill of them behind their backs.

4. In the eyes of his parents, his talent for music is even greater than Mozart's.

5. The two countries have similar cultural origins.

6. All his companions gave up and backed out, but he kept his chin up and forged on.

7. Maybe you have no idea what Costco is, but in the United States it's a household name.

8. You won't find a place to worship in the willage— there is nothing remotely resembling a chapel.

9. His classmates go to him for help with any math questions they have; they think he's the best of the best.

10. He is indifferent to everything but his own interests.

11. Outer space is a place devoid of everything but extreme coldness, darkness and silence.

12. After some trial and error, I finally came to a rough understanding of what it was all about.

13. She felt it was a bargain. She had haggled back and forth over the price for almost half an hour.

14. As the introduction of the distinguished guests dragged on and on, some people in the audience began to yawn and groan.

15. Suddenly a wonderful idea occurred to (struck) me, and I couldn't wait to tell my friends about it.

16. I made repeated checks of the doors and windows for fear that someone might break in.

17. He was so absorbed in (reading) the magazine that he didn't even notice me coming in.

18. Friends hailing from our sister city were each presented with a bagful of souvenirs.

19. I know being habitually late is a bad habit; I will try my best to break it.

20. A class captain is supposed to be in charge of keeping the whole class running efficiently.

21. A brief interview with him was enough to tell that he's the best candidate for the post.

22. No one can see their misery without feeling sick at heart.

23. Most of the furniture had been moved into the house, but a small part

of it had to be left exposed to the elements because of the limited space within.

24. We happened to be right in the middle of the typhoon's expected path, so we were warned we should evacuate to a safer place.

25. Having been spoiled rotten by his grandparents, the child is a headache in the eyes of his teachers.

26. The first typhoon didn't strike the island, nor will the one that has developed near Guam.

27. Her swollen face and her tale of being abused tore at my heart.

28. The people in the ghetto are clothed in rags and housed in slums.

29. He works very hard, but he does not even have a house to call his own.

30. He not only donates money, but volunteers as well.

Linking English

讀李家同學英文1：我的盲人恩師

2006年10月初版　　　　　　　　　　　定價：新臺幣250元
2016年4月初版第八刷
有著作權・翻印必究
Printed in Taiwan.

著　　　者	李	家	同		
譯　　　者	Nick Hawkins				
解　　　析	周	正	一		
總　編　輯	胡	金	倫		
總　經　理	羅	國	俊		
發　行　人	林	載	爵		

出　版　者	聯經出版事業股份有限公司	叢書主編	何　采　嬪
地　　　址	台北市基隆路一段180號4樓	校　　對	Nick Hawkins
台北聯經書房	台北市新生南路三段94號		林　慧　如
電　　話	(0 2) 2 3 6 2 0 3 0 8	封面設計	翁　國　鈞
台中分公司	台中市北區崇德路一段198號		
暨門市電話	(0 4) 2 2 3 1 2 0 2 3		
郵政劃撥帳戶第0100559-3號			
郵撥電話	(0 2) 2 3 6 2 0 3 0 8		
印　刷　者	文聯彩色製版印刷有限公司		
總　經　銷	聯合發行股份有限公司		
發　行　所	新北市新店區寶橋路235巷6弄6號2F		
電　　話	(0 2) 2 9 1 7 8 0 2 2		

行政院新聞局出版事業登記證局版臺業字第0130號

本書如有缺頁，破損，倒裝請寄回台北聯經書房更換。　ISBN　978-957-08-3066-8 (平裝)
聯經網址 http://www.linkingbooks.com.tw
電子信箱 e-mail:linking@udngroup.com

國家圖書館出版品預行編目資料

讀李家同學英文 1：我的盲人恩師 /
李家同著 . Nick Hawkins 譯 . 周正一解析 .
初版 . 臺北市：聯經，2006 年（民 95）
224 面；14.8×21 公分 .（Linking English）
ISBN　978-957-08-3066-8（平裝）
[2016年4月初版第八刷]

1. 英國語言 - 讀本

805.18　　　　　　　　　　　　　95018875

從國人的需求出發的英文學習書

糾正中國人最容易犯錯的基本文法

專門替中國人寫的
英文基本文法

李家同、海柏◎ 合著

定價200元

如果你覺得，坊間的文法書太難了：讀完後文法還是不好；如果你真的想打下深厚的文法基礎，可是卻苦無門路，那麼，這本書就適合你。因為這本書是針對中國人最容易犯的文法錯誤所編寫的書！

我們兩人都有過教初級英文的經驗，我們發現我們中國人寫英文句子時，會犯獨特的錯誤，比方說，我們常將兩個動詞連在一起用，我們也會將動詞用成名詞，我們對過去式和現在式毫無觀念。更加不要說現在完成式了。而天生講英文的人是不可能犯這種錯的。

我們這本英文文法書，是專門為中國人寫的。以下是這本書的一些特徵：我們一開始就強調一些英文文法的基本規定，這些規定都是我們中國人所不太習慣的。也就是說，我們一開始就告訴了讀者，大家不要犯這種錯誤。

我們馬上就進入動詞，理由很簡單，這是我們中國人最弱的地方。根據我們的經驗，絕大多數的錯誤，都與動詞有關。這也難怪，中文裡面，哪有什麼動詞的規則？

最後我們要勸告初學的讀者，你們應該多多做練習，練習做多了，你自然不會犯錯。總有一天，你說英文的時候，動詞該加s，你就會加s。該用過去式，就會用過去式。兩個動詞也不會連在一起用，疑問句也會用疑問句的語法。那是多麼美好的一天。希望這一天早日到來！

李家同

海　柏

聯經出版事業公司

www.linkingbooks.com.tw

郵政劃撥帳號：01005593　戶名：聯經出版事業公司

洽詢電話：02-2641-8662

聯經出版公司信用卡訂購單

信用卡別： ☐VISA CARD ☐MASTER CARD ☐聯合信用卡

訂購人姓名： ＿＿＿＿＿＿＿＿＿＿＿＿＿＿＿＿＿＿＿＿

訂購日期： ＿＿＿＿＿＿年＿＿＿＿＿月＿＿＿＿＿日

信用卡號： ＿＿＿＿＿＿ ＿＿＿＿＿ ＿＿＿＿＿ ＿＿＿＿＿

信用卡簽名： ＿＿＿＿＿＿＿＿＿＿＿＿＿＿(與信用卡上簽名同)

信用卡有效期限： ＿＿＿＿＿＿年＿＿＿＿＿月止

聯絡電話： 日(O)＿＿＿＿＿＿＿＿夜(H)＿＿＿＿＿＿＿＿

聯絡地址： ☐ ☐☐＿＿＿＿＿＿＿＿＿＿＿＿＿＿＿＿＿＿＿

訂購金額： 新台幣＿＿＿＿＿＿＿＿＿＿＿＿＿＿＿＿＿元整
（訂購金額 500 元以下，請加付掛號郵資 50 元）

發票： ☐二聯式 ☐三聯式

發票抬頭： ＿＿＿＿＿＿＿＿＿＿＿＿＿＿＿＿＿＿＿

統一編號： ＿＿＿＿＿＿＿＿＿＿＿＿＿＿＿＿＿＿＿

發票地址： ＿＿＿＿＿＿＿＿＿＿＿＿＿＿＿＿＿＿＿

如收件人或收件地址不同時，請填：

收件人姓名： ☐先生
＿＿＿＿＿＿＿＿＿＿＿＿＿＿＿＿＿＿ ☐小姐

聯絡電話： 日(O)＿＿＿＿＿＿＿＿夜(H)＿＿＿＿＿＿＿＿

收貨地址： ＿＿＿＿＿＿＿＿＿＿＿＿＿＿＿＿＿＿＿

· 茲訂購下列書種‧帳款由本人信用卡帳戶支付 ·

書名	數量	單價	合計
		總計	

訂購辦法填妥後

直接傳真 FAX：(02)8692-1268 或(02)2648-7859

洽詢專線：(02)26418662 或(02)26422629 轉 241

網上訂購，請上聯經網站： www.linkingbooks.com.tw